"If I'm not with you every minute of the night, you might fall into danger again," Luc said.

The pulse in her throat, her scent, her lips, her eyes...everything about Dani woke his most atavistic primal needs and desires. Much as she despised vampires, she had no idea of the pleasures he could show her, the absolute heaven that lay between life and death.

But *he* knew, and it made him both restless and dangerous. The need for action filled him—the only antidote to desire.

The room was too small to truly escape. Worse, he could smell moments of desire passing through her, too. They came and went like waves on a shore, as she battled them down. What was it about her?

Books by Rachel Lee

Harlequin Nocturne

****Claim the Night* #127
****Claimed by a Vampire* #129
****Forever Claimed* #131

Harlequin Romantic Suspense

***The Final Mission* #1655
***Just a Cowboy* #1663
***The Rescue Pilot* #1671

Silhouette Romantic Suspense

An Officer and a Gentleman #370
Serious Risks #394
Defying Gravity #430
**Exile's End* #449
**Cherokee Thunder* #463
**Miss Emmaline and the Archangel* #482
**Ironheart* #494
**Lost Warriors* #535
**Point of No Return* #566
**A Question of Justice* #613
**Nighthawk* #781
**Cowboy Comes Home* #865
**Involuntary Daddy* #955
Holiday Heroes #1487
"*A Soldier for All Seasons*"
***A Soldier's Homecoming* #1519
***Protector of One* #1555
***The Unexpected Hero* #1567
***The Man from Nowhere* #1595
***Her Hero in Hiding* #1611
***A Soldier's Redemption* #1635
***No Ordinary Hero* #1643

*Conard County
**Conard County:
The Next Generation
***The Claiming

RACHEL LEE

was hooked on writing by the age of twelve, and practiced her craft as she moved from place to place all over the United States. This *New York Times* bestselling author now resides in Florida and has the joy of writing full-time.

FOREVER CLAIMED

RACHEL LEE

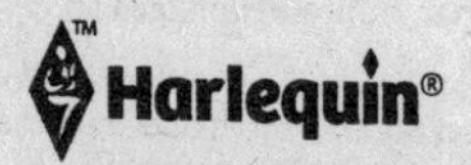

TORONTO NEW YORK LONDON
AMSTERDAM PARIS SYDNEY HAMBURG
STOCKHOLM ATHENS TOKYO MILAN MADRID
PRAGUE WARSAW BUDAPEST AUCKLAND

Recycling programs
for this product may
not exist in your area.

ISBN-13: 978-0-373-61878-1

FOREVER CLAIMED

This edition published by arrangement with Harlequin Books S.A.

For questions and comments about the quality of this book please contact us at Customer_eCare@Harlequin.ca.

www.Harlequin.com

Printed in U.S.A.

Dear Reader,

Forever Claimed provided me with an opportunity to take a different look at werewolves. I like taking different looks at things.

Our heroine, Dani, is a werewolf who can't shape-shift and has left her clan because she can't stand being different. She was also raised with a deep loathing of vampires, so imagine her shock when she discovers her life was saved by a vampire named Luc.

Against a backdrop of a war between vampires, Dani must choose a side. It is a sometimes painful journey, especially when she finds herself increasingly attracted to a vampire, one of her family's eternal enemies.

Dani's journey of self-discovery leads her to some strange and dangerous places and finally to the one place she belongs—in the arms of a vampire.

Enjoy!

Rachel

Chapter 1

He smelled blood on the night air. Little did he guess the danger it was about to lead him into.

Luc St. Just sped through the dark city streets, moving shadow to shadow, too fast for human eyes to see. He didn't want to be here. Indeed, he was returning to this place only because he felt he owed at least a small favor to Jude Messenger, a fellow vampire. Jude was one of very few vampires he counted as a friend.

Which wasn't saying much. For most of his two centuries as a vampire, Luc had grown truly close to only one other of his kind: Natasha. His lost lover, his claimed mate. When she had died, madness had overtaken him, and although with Jude's help he'd achieved a measure of vengeance, the excruciating sense of loss and sorrow still remained.

A claiming was supposed to be broken by vengeance, but apparently it hadn't been. That left only his own death to release him. But for some reason he clung to his existence, however unwillingly. He hadn't yet asked a vampire for mercy, although he had come close. So he was still here, and because some dregs of conscience prompted him, he was entering a city he had no desire to ever see again.

He should be in Paris, the city of his heart. Or anywhere in Europe where life felt more comfortable than this new world with all its brashness and noise.

But all those thoughts, thoughts that dogged his heels almost obsessively—a sign of a claiming—dropped into the background as he smelled blood on the air.

He was a vampire, and there was no sweeter siren call than that of fresh blood. He lifted his head, sniffing the air, locating the direction from which the enticing scent came. The park. Someone had been injured badly.

He could have just continued on his way, but the call was hard to resist, and his resistance was low these days. If nothing else, he could at least put some human out of misery. Or so he thought, trying to put a noble veneer on what was an irresistible instinct.

Even he could see some bleak humor in his own rationalization.

He slipped through the shadowy woods swiftly, the night as clear to him as day would have been to a human. A high, full moon deepened the shadows, allowing him to pass swiftly, invisible to human eyes, just another shadow among shadows. But for him, colors shone with jewellike brilliance.

The night came alive to him in ways it never would for a mortal. The movement of every leaf, the insects crawling in the grass or nibbling on leaves, he could hear all that. Even the sound of water running up inside the trunks of trees reached him with a delightful syncopated rhythm. He heard a bird's wings flutter then settle quickly.

The night sang to him.

He could hear the distant sound of a baby's cry, a couple of people who argued blocks away and even the sound of someone's private lovemaking.

Once, he had soaked up these sounds with pleasure. No more, for he had lost his capacity for pleasure. Tonight he shoved them into the background as the call of blood dominated.

He paused a few times, testing the air, smelling for humans. What he smelled gave him pause. As the delicious scent of fresh blood grew, so did another scent: the scent of his own kind.

"Putain," he said under his breath. He should clear out now. He had a message to deliver, and a face-down with some hungry vampires enjoying their meal would not serve him at all. But there was too much blood on the air, too much to be a simple

feeding. What if those he had come to warn Jude about had already arrived?

Even when not concerned, a vampire tended to be very quiet, but now he heightened his senses and moved with true stealth to avoid his own kind. Trees zipped past him. He stayed off the paved paths and tasted the air frequently. Both the scent of blood and vampires grew, but the blood strengthened more quickly. Whoever had done this thing, he judged they had moved on.

He picked up his pace a bit, then saw the heat signature of a body lying on the ground amidst the trees. The sound of a too-rapid heartbeat reached him. The victim. He circled quickly, looking for others of his kind and soon detected they had moved on to the south.

He and the food were alone.

He crept toward her and what he saw appalled even him. He was no saint, despite his name, and indulged in willing mortal blood without compunction. But this was not a willing donation, and the savagery of the attack on the woman lying before him shrieked unnecessary violence. She must have put up one hell of a fight and paid for it with a torn and possibly broken body.

Her heartbeat raced as her body fought to pump its diminishing blood supply to essential organs. She hovered on the brink of death, and he wondered why her attackers hadn't finished her. It would have been so easy for them to just snap her neck.

And what that said about the attackers offended him. There was no need to have been this violent or to have left the woman to die slowly. Like many hunters, he believed in clean kills. Vampires were not cats, to maul their prey. They had other ways of satisfying those urges, sexual and seductive ways that needn't lead to this kind of mess.

This group had left a message, writ clear on the woman's body.

He could have put an end to her suffering right then, but stayed himself. She might be just the proof he needed to convince Jude of the gravity and reality of the warning he carried.

Just as he was bending toward her, he caught an unmistakable smell on the breeze. He straightened and whirled just in time to see another vampire seeping out of the shadows toward him.

He considered, then said, "Is she yours?"

"I came back to finish her." The other vampire, short and wiry, paused. "You can finish her if you want."

Luc wanted but refused to, however easy it would have been. "You were a trifle rough on her. She isn't very appealing just now."

The other shrugged and moved closer. "Four of us, and she fought. She was quite a handful. In any event, I thought by now she'd be weak enough to finish. Apparently so."

"She'll be dead soon enough."

"So finish her."

He heard the challenge, realized this was one of the rogues and he was being asked to choose a side. If he didn't finish the woman, he would be considered an enemy.

How odd, thought a detached part of his mind. A very odd conversation for two vampires to have, especially when they had never met before.

There were four of them altogether, useful information. He lifted his head, tasting the air, but could detect no others anywhere near.

"All right," he said.

It was enough to make the other relax just a bit. Enough to give him the opportunity to spring. While he had little advantage in strength, he had another advantage: years of training with the épée had made him fast, springy and, oh, so deadly when it came to one on one.

The knife was out of his pocket in an instant and buried in the other swiftly. He pulled it upward, until it reached the heart. He stared into eyes gone black as night, heard the gurgle of the other's breath. Then, with no compunction whatever, he pulled the knife free, dropped it and reached for the other's head. A second later he heard the satisfying crack and the other fell dead. Dawn would take care of his remains.

Too easy, he thought. Entirely too easy. Either the other was a total fool, or he had honestly believed that any unknown vampire would not hesitate to take his leftovers. That said more about the rogues than anything he'd heard so far.

He picked up his knife, wiping it on the other's clothes, tucking it away. He froze, taking in the night air and listening. No others were about. Not yet. But he had to move fast.

Picking up the blood-soaked woman was hard. Not because she was heavy—his preternatural strength made her feel little heavier than air—nor because she was covered in blood. The difficulty came from the way the blood called to him, begging him to drink. It would have been easy, so easy, to drain this woman and walk away. In fact, nothing would have satisfied him more.

But he might need her.

Still, he hesitated. If he took her with him, she'd leave a trail as clear as neon on the night air, clear to noses that could smell it. If it crossed the path of the rogue vampires, he might have more trouble than he could handle.

With a sigh he lifted the woman higher into his arms. It wasn't as if he was attached to his existence. If this turned out to be the end, he wouldn't exactly be disappointed.

Nor would he be able to blame himself for failing to warn Jude.

Shrugging slightly, he took off through the woods effortlessly, the woman seeming light as eiderdown.

He changed one thing, though. He chose a more circuitous route to Jude's place, so that if others caught the scent on the breeze they should assume he was merely carrying away prey to a safer location.

With his arms full, he couldn't scale any buildings, so he was forced to stick with ground streets. The limitation made him edgy. He hated to feel edgy. Normally he felt so secure in his power and strength that he seldom spared his own safety a thought.

All of that was changing. The world was changing, right now, tonight. The only question was how far he wanted to involve himself in that change.

Oddly enough, he didn't know. He had been sure when he set out for Jude, but something about the savaged body in his arms filled him with doubts. As if her silent testimony to the very thing Jude was fighting made him part of the fight.

Not now, he told himself. *Just get the woman to Jude as proof of what is coming. Think about the rest later.*

He paused several times, checking the air, but there was no sign he was being followed. Then he noticed that the woman's heart had slowed dangerously and that she no longer leaked blood. Minutes from death probably, but still evidence.

He quickened his pace, now making a straight beeline for Jude. He didn't want to sort through his tangled feelings just then, told himself he wanted to get the woman to Jude so Jude could decide what to do with her. Save her, let her die, kill her. He didn't care.

But somewhere inside his aching, sorrowful, almost deadened heart, a voice whispered otherwise. He tried to quash it, knowing it could only cause trouble. It rose again, however, a little louder.

And the pressure of it made him run even faster.

Jude lived in his office, a place slightly below street level with the kind of security a spy agency might have envied. Because of it, he had to press the button and look into a camera.

Then he heard a familiar voice: Chloe, Jude's assistant. A human who had cause to loathe him.

"Well, look what the cat dragged in," her voice drawled over the speaker. Then a note of horror canceled her sarcasm. "My God, St. Just, what did you do?"

Evidently she could see his burden. "Nothing but try to save this mortal. I need to see Jude now. Let me in."

He heard the sound of a buzzer. Adjusting his hold on the woman, he reached for the door and opened it.

The hallway was dark as always, out of deference to Jude's vampire eyes. Spilling from a doorway, however, was warm lamplight: the entry to the inner offices where Chloe ruled the roost when Jude wasn't there to keep her in line.

He crossed the threshold, narrowing his eyes

against the sudden light, and laid the woman on the couch. He ignored Chloe's gasp.

He turned to look at her. "Jude," he repeated.

Chloe was a piece of work, and she had plenty of reason to despise him. Just last year he had kidnapped her briefly and she'd taken it in her usual manner: with sarcastic anger.

She stood now glaring at him, her hands on her hips. Her hair was still dyed the deepest of blacks, heavy black makeup outlined her eyes, and her costume managed to bridge the territory between stripper and punk: lots of black leather and lace with black leggings that barely protected her modesty.

Sometimes Luc missed the beautiful gowns women had worn in the old days. The modern version of fashion didn't appeal to him at all. It left too little to the imagination.

"You're not going to tell me you didn't do that," she said, accusing him with a pointed finger.

"If I had done this," he said stonily, "I would not have brought her here, and certainly not still alive. Jude," he demanded again.

Chloe bit her scarlet-painted lower lip, the only color on her except for a blood-colored ruby ring. "He and Terri are out on a date. What do you expect him to do about her, anyway?" she demanded, waving a hand at the woman.

"I expect him to listen to a warning I have to give him. That's proof of the danger he's in."

Chloe's eyes widened a shade. "You better not be lying, St. Just."

The man he had been before would have considered those fighting words. The man he had discovered after Natasha's death couldn't deny she had a right to speak them.

"Jude, now," he repeated. "Then we can decide what to do with this mortal."

"It looks too late to me," Chloe muttered, but she pulled out a cell phone from a skirt so layered with black lace and net that it stuck out from her body almost like a tutu, and then pressed a button before placing it to her ear.

"Sorry, boss," she said into the receiver. "St. Just is here with a woman who looks like she's been half butchered and he says you're in danger. He wants to see you now."

She ended the call and scowled at him. "You *so* better not be lying."

He didn't bother to argue with her or say another word. With Chloe, he'd swiftly learned, you could waste a lot of breath. Instead, he just glided over to an armchair and sat, folding his arms.

The outer office hadn't changed in any important way; Jude's inner sanctum still lay behind a locked door, a deceptively ordinary-looking door. He scanned his environs because it was native instinct to be aware of his surroundings, not because they interested him. He looked everywhere except at the woman on the couch.

Five minutes later, he heard the sounds of Jude and Terri coming down the hall. From the speed of their arrival, he guessed Jude must have carried Terri on his back and traveled at top speed. Terri, clad in evening dress covered by a heavy parka, looked windblown.

As they crossed the threshold, their gazes fixed on the woman on the couch. Terri's bright blue eyes widened, and she sped across the room with a rustle of sapphire silk to kneel beside the victim. As a forensic pathologist, she was also a trained doctor.

"My God," she whispered. "She's almost dead."

"She's been almost dead since I found her."

Jude, dressed as always in elegantly tailored black beneath a long black leather coat, looked at Luc. "What happened?"

"Vampires." Luc shrugged. "I could smell them in the area. But the woman is just evidence, Jude. I came to warn you. There are those who don't like the way you drove them out of this city, who don't like your rules about not harming humans. They're coming back to take vengeance, they're bringing others who feel as they do. And from what was done to that—" he waved toward the woman on the couch "—I suspect they may already be here."

"That," Chloe interjected sarcastically, "is a human being."

Luc shrugged. None of this was his problem, beyond delivering his warning so Jude could prepare. He had done what he set out to do, and could leave.

Except for some reason he didn't. He just kept sitting there, almost as if waiting for something.

"I should get her to the hospital," Terri said, her fingertips pressed to the woman's throat. She hadn't even yet removed her jacket. "I don't know if there's time, but she needs a transfusion, a lot of stitches, maybe even surgery, depending."

"There isn't time," Jude said with unusual gentleness. "Trust me. I sense it. She'll be gone in a couple of minutes."

Terri swore softly and settled back on her heels. "Do you know how much it goes against my grain to sit by while someone dies?"

"Do you want me to try to turn her?" Jude asked. "There might be just enough time."

Terri's blue eyes fixed on him. "You'd turn a stranger, but not me?"

"She's a stranger. I love *you.* I don't want to make you something you might regret for eternity."

Terri simply shook her head, apparently having no retort.

Luc watched as Jude went to place a hand on his human mate's shoulder. "Trust me, Terri, this woman is better off dying. I know what it's like to be turned without a choice. Without knowing and understanding."

Luc was the last person to argue that being a vampire was good. He was suffering the torments of the damned because of a vampire trait he'd been unable to escape: claiming. The beauty of a claiming was undeniable. But so was the obsession, and the madness that followed if you lost what you had claimed. He wouldn't wish that on anyone, not even his worst enemy.

Jude turned to him, his golden eyes intent. "So they're coming after me? And you think they're already here?"

"I think this *woman*—" he emphasized the word for Chloe's benefit "—is the opening salvo, if you will."

"Do you know what their plan is?"

"A reign of terror designed to draw you out in such a way that they can terminate you."

"They could just come knock on my door."

"But what fun would that be?"

Chloe shuddered. "I knew there was a reason I don't like most vampires."

Luc ignored her, knowing full well he was the reason she didn't like other vampires. Her liking for Jude and for his friend Creed was obvious enough. He didn't care. Chloe was just another human, low on his radar of importance.

"They are going to take over the city," he said. "They are either going to kill you or make it impossible for you to remain here. One way or another, they'll sabotage the authority you've been exercising in this city. They'll make sure another vampire never heeds your rules."

"I'm not the only one with those rules."

"True, *mon ami,* but this group is completely

rogue and they've been whipped up by some of those you forced out of this city in the past. You're just the first target among what I suspect will be many."

Jude leaned back against Chloe's desk and folded his arms. "I don't have to tell you, Luc. Most of us have always tried to avoid creating situations that draw attention to our existence."

Luc nodded. "I have helped remove rogues before. A certain amount of careful coexistence is necessary. All-out war between vampires and humans would benefit neither of our kinds. But that is what this group wishes."

Chloe spoke. "Why the hell should *you* care?"

Jude spoke, silencing her. "Have you never thought, Chloe, what would happen to my kind if there were no food left?"

Luc knew a moment of dark amusement as Chloe's expression changed. Evidently she didn't think of herself as a food group. But why would she when Jude restricted himself almost entirely to blood from blood banks? She probably hadn't thought about where all that blood came from.

Suddenly Terri gasped. Luc looked at her and saw her face filled with astonishment. "She's healing," she said. "My God, her wounds are closing."

Jude bent swiftly over the woman and looked. "You're right. No ordinary human." He straightened and looked at Luc. "What did you bring into my home?"

Apprehension chilled Luc, the first he had felt

in a long time. Rising, he moved swiftly to look at the woman. Her clothes were still blood soaked and ripped, but he could see that her wounds had closed just since he brought her here.

"I don't know," he said. "*Mon dieu,* I don't know."

"Hell," said Chloe, who always had two cents to add. "If it's not vampire and it's not human, then what the devil is it?"

Dani Makar woke suddenly, knowing she wasn't alone. Worse, the first thing to assault her nose was the smell of vampires. She kept her eyes closed and tried to maintain a slow, steady rhythm in her heartbeat, even though she knew it was probably useless. Those bloodsuckers would have smelled it, heard it, the instant she awoke.

But she tried to keep up the pretense anyway, hoping against hope. She knew what had attacked her. What she couldn't figure out was why she was lying on something soft instead of the hard ground, and why she smelled humans, as well.

She hurt from head to toe, but knew that would pass quickly. Despite all the things she had failed to inherit from her family, she had inherited two things: an acute sense of smell and quick healing from wounds.

She'd also inherited a loathing for bloodsuckers, one which had been amply proved in the park. Now, as near as she could tell, they held her captive. She expected no mercy from their kind.

Waiting for the instant she could no longer pretend to be unconscious, she tried to figure out how many were in the room. Listening, she was sure she heard two females and two males, though she couldn't tell which of them were vampire and which were human. Her nose was clouded with their scents.

The presence of humans and vampires together didn't shock her. She had been taught about the hypnotic effect vampires had on humans. What she didn't know was whether she was susceptible. She had, after all, been forced to resign herself to life as a normal without *being* fully normal.

But after the attack that had nearly killed her, why would they want to keep her captive now? It didn't make sense.

"She's awake," said a deep voice.

Then she heard a rustle and smelled the odor of human come closer.

"Can you open your eyes?" a woman's gentle voice asked.

"Stand back," said the same deep voice. "We don't know what she is or how she'll react."

That gave Dani her opening. If they were wary of her, she might be able to take advantage of it.

Instantly she sprang up into a crouch and snarled, her gaze moving from one to the other. Even as she did it, she knew how pathetic she must look, like a puppy pretending to be a full-grown wolf. But maybe it would be enough.

"It's all right," the familiar woman's voice said.

Dani glanced at her, taking in a tiny, dark-haired beauty wearing a sapphire cocktail dress. Her expression was kind. The other woman regarded her with consternation from eyes surrounded in entirely too much makeup.

Then there were the men. In an instant she knew they were the vampires. One wore neatly tailored black and stood leaning against a desk. The other was seated and also wore black, though he looked a bit more disheveled. And like too many vampires, they were handsome, almost as if their change transformed them into objects of dark beauty.

"We rescued you," said the blond vampire, his voice slightly accented. "I found you in the park and brought you here."

Dani gave him another snarl. Like she was going to believe a bloodsucker?

For long seconds, no one moved. Then the elegant man with the dark hair said, "You can leave if you'd like. I'll show you the door."

She doubted that and didn't move. Besides, she hurt all over and wasn't yet sure how far she could walk. Her clothes were torn and covered in blood. She wouldn't make it far before the police stopped her, and then she'd have to make up some lie about what had happened because normals absolutely didn't believe in vampires, and she didn't want to get committed.

"It's all right," the woman in blue said again, her voice remaining gentle. She moved closer and Dani smelled vampire all over her, but also the scent of human. She might be in league with the bloodsuckers, but she was still a normal.

The woman edged onto the couch beside her, moving slowly.

"Terri," said the dark vampire warningly.

"It's all right, Jude. She's frightened. After the way she was attacked, how could she be anything else?"

The woman called Terri smiled at her. "I'm Terri, and I'm a doctor. I'm both amazed and thankful at the way you healed. We thought we couldn't save you."

Dani didn't answer, choosing to reveal nothing.

"I'll give you something to wear so you can leave. I'm afraid my clothes might be a bit small on you, but at least they'll cover you so you don't have to answer questions."

Fear immediately spiked Dani. How could this woman know she didn't want to answer questions? Then the answer came to her: she had healed too fast from nearly fatal injuries. Of course they knew she might have something to hide.

Uneasier than ever, she edged away and adjusted her crouch, ready to spring if necessary. One hand felt for and found her necklace, the crystal wolf's head that hung by a leather thong around her neck. It was all she had left of her old life, and her heart squeezed with relief when she realized she still had it. It had been her last gift from her mother, and she would probably never receive another. She drew a steadying breath and refocused on her enemies.

Then the blond vampire with the faint accent spoke. "My advice would be to remain here until just before dawn. There are rogues on the streets, the ones who attacked you. You don't want to encounter them again."

Dani finally spoke. "How do I know it wasn't you, vampire? You and your friend?"

Instantly she wished she could recall the words. She had just revealed too much, that she could tell they were bloodsuckers, and in so doing had made herself a threat to them.

"Très intéressant," said the blond one, revealing the source of his accent. "She knows what we are. So she must be able to smell us."

"I can smell you, all right," Dani said forcefully, hoping to hold them at bay with a show of strength, however false. "Your stench fills the room."

"So you know what we are. Perhaps you can tell us what *you* are."

"I'm a human," Dani said, catching herself just before she revealed more by saying she was a normal. "Can't you smell it, bloodsucker?"

He shrugged and turned his head away from her, as if losing interest. That offended her, that he considered her such a small threat he could ignore her. Even if it was true.

The woman, Terri, reached out and touched her gently on the arm. Dani pulled back.

"Let me explain some things," Terri said. "That man over there? That's Jude, and he's my husband. Whatever you may think about vampires, he doesn't condone what happened to you, and now I'll have to endure the anxiety while he sets out to hunt those who hurt you."

Almost in spite of herself, Dani looked at her. "What are you talking about?"

"Jude," said the other woman, "is a bit of an avenger. He usually deals with demons, but now I'm *quite* sure he's going to look for the rogues who attacked you."

"Chloe," the dark one called Jude said in a warning tone.

"Well, it's true, boss. Besides, you're not going to be able to avoid looking for them, not with the news that St. Just brought us."

Jude frowned at her, but said nothing.

The blond one suddenly rose and in an instant was bent over, his face inches from hers. His black-as-ebony gaze was mesmerizing, and the only way she could fight it was to pull back as far as possible.

"She's human," he said, "but not quite. I don't care what you are, *ma cocotte,* but I know what you were used for. You were attacked on purpose. You are a declaration of war against Jude and any other vampire who forswears harm to humans. It was simply your misfortune to be there when they decided to make the declaration. But I will tell you this, they are still out there, still hunting to create more mayhem. Since you healed, you can now attract them once again. Especially since you reek of blood."

Her heart skittered, and she found herself wondering what to believe.

"Stay here until dawn. Then go home and stay there, because the attack on you is a mere taste of what these rogues intend to inflict on this entire city."

"Why should I believe you?"

He shrugged and drew away. "I don't care what you believe. I don't even care what you do. I did what I needed to, I brought you to Jude to prove these rogues have arrived. Beyond that..." He shrugged.

He seemed about ready to walk out the door, then he settled in the chair once again, looking angry and despairing all at once.

Dani had to drag her gaze away, appalled that she found him so magnetic. A bloodsucker magnetic? Every fiber of her being rebelled. It came as a relief when she looked at the one called Jude and realized she didn't feel the same pull toward him. So she wasn't utterly lost.

"How about some introductions," Jude said. "I'm Jude Messenger, and you're in my office. Terri already told you she's my wife. This other lady is Chloe, my assistant. And that's Luc St. Just, the one who brought you here and came to tell me the rogues are on the march. And you are?"

She hesitated, then decided to see where this led.

They had already told her she could leave. Did they really mean it?

"Dani Makar," she said.

"Nice to meet you, Dani Makar," Jude said. The two women echoed him. Luc, on the other hand, seemed to have sunk into a dark mood. He made no acknowledgment at all.

"Luc was right," Chloe said. "Much as I hate to admit it." She shot daggers his way, but Luc appeared oblivious. "You're safer going home at dawn. If vampires are going to fight, mere mortals don't want to be in the way."

"But why should they fight?" Dani asked. Something was askew here and she wanted to understand it. Having been attacked once, she needed to know enough to protect herself. "You're all the same."

At that, Jude laughed. A genuine laugh. "That's about as true of us as it is of mortals. Some of us don't believe in harming humans. Others of us would rather not control our impulses."

Chloe spoke again. "About seven years ago, Jude drove a group of vampires out of town because they, um..." She hesitated.

"Overindulged?" Jude suggested with heavy sarcasm.

"I guess you could call it that. And from what Luc tells us, they've come back for vengeance. They may even want to start a war between Jude's kind of vampire and the ones who just take whatever they want."

"But why should you care what you do to humans?"

At that moment Luc rejoined the conversation. "It's simple. Life is ever so much easier for us if no one believes we exist. And the only way to ensure that is never to take what we want unless it is offered freely."

This was an entirely new view of vampires, and Dani was reluctant to swallow it whole. "So you wouldn't have attacked me the way they did?"

"Not I," said Jude, firmly.

"Nor I," said Luc, his black eyes burning. "Not unless you wanted it."

"Why would anyone want that?"

"You'd be surprised what some people want," Luc said flatly. Then he stood so quickly Dani hardly saw him move.

"Jude, I must dine."

At once Jude straightened and led him toward the door on the wall near the couch. He punched in a code quickly on a keypad, then swiped a card. Only then did he push the door open. The two vampires disappeared inside, leaving the three women alone.

"Dine?" Dani repeated.

No one answered her. Not a soul.

Fear shuddered through her again. Her voice smaller than she would have liked, she finally said, "I'll take those clothes."

She needed to get away. Now.

Chapter 2

Jude pulled a bag of blood out of the refrigerator in his office and passed it to Luc. He also put out a glass in case Luc didn't want to drink from the bag.

Luc looked at the glass, remembering the times he had drunk blood from fine crystal goblets. Times spent with Natasha.

"What's the story?" Jude asked.

"I told you."

"No, I meant with you. Vengeance didn't help you?"

"It rid me of the anger."

"But not the rest of it." Jude settled on a chair behind his desk, facing Luc across it. Luc finally seated himself and bit the bag open. He hesitated, then decided not to use a glass, not to remind himself of Natasha through such a simple thing. He drained the bag flat in seconds, then passed it back to Jude, who tossed it into a biohazard container.

They faced each other across the desk, Jude clearly waiting, Luc reluctant to speak. Yet he couldn't blame Jude for his curiosity. Few enough vampires emerged on the other side of claiming, and he must certainly have been curious about it.

"The world is still bleak," he said finally. "I may ask you for mercy."

Jude lifted one brow. "I hope you don't."

"It would be your obligation." It was one obligation all vampires respected: if one of their kind could take this life no longer, a request for mercy—death—was always honored.

"Don't ask it of me," Jude said. "I need you."

"For this fight?" Luc sounded almost scornful. "I don't care anymore, Jude. I gave you the warning because I felt I owed it to you. If vampires want to destroy each other, why should I care?"

"You used to care. And maybe your problem right now is that you're not allowing yourself to care about anything. You're wallowing, Luc."

The rage that flashed through Luc just then almost made him leap across the desk and attack Jude. He gripped the arms of his chair until his fingers buried themselves in the leather and then the padding beneath. "How would you know what I am going through?" The words emerged from between his clenched teeth.

"You're right, I don't know," Jude replied calmly. "But I know what you used to be. What I see before me now is a man who won't let go."

"I can't let go."

"Perhaps not." Jude sighed. "If you want to die, at least die doing something important. Don't make it pointless by asking me to break your neck."

The tension between them nearly made the air sizzle. But then Luc released his anger, acknowledging that it was misdirected. Jude wasn't his problem. An interrupted claiming was his problem. Weariness was his problem.

"I'll think about it."

"Thank you." Jude leaned forward and drummed his fingers on the desktop. "I should probably just take Terri and run. If there's going to be a bloodbath, she's my first concern."

"It would be the wise thing, but I've noted you often avoid the easiest course."

Jude flashed a brief smile. "It looks that way."

Luc shook his head. "Oh, you always have a reason for what you do, *mon ami.* Battling demons, fighting your own kind. Most would call that insane."

"I call it necessary."

"Which is exactly why you won't flee." Luc released his grip on the chair arms and crossed his legs. "And you have a problem now in your office."

"When do I not?"

One corner of Luc's mouth twitched upward.

"True. But this one is intriguing. She can't be human."

"Not fully, in any event. That much is clear."

"We—or you, actually—must now concern ourselves with whether she might be an additional threat. She *smells* human, however, or I would not have brought her here."

"I agree about her aroma. She certainly doesn't smell like anything *else* I've ever met." He drummed his fingers again briefly. "Well, she's certainly not in league with the rogues. I doubt even someone who heals as swiftly as she does would have volunteered to be treated like that."

"I agree. So now let us go learn what we can."

The blood he had drunk had energized him, cold and nearly lifeless as it was. Things didn't look quite as bleak as they had when he'd arrived here hungry. But they were still bleak.

Natasha's death had left a gaping hole in his heart, his mind, his life, and he was sure he would never be able to fill it.

But for now, he decided, perhaps Jude was right. If he was going to choose death, he might as well die fighting. The idea better suited his nature. Maybe that was why he had hesitated to take the final step for so long: the notion of leaving quietly just didn't fit him. A death in battle...well, there was something to be said for that.

Dani had showered and changed into a pair of too-tight, too-short jeans and a baggy sweatshirt that

Chloe and Terri had managed to find for her. She still huddled in a corner of the couch but no longer looked ready to spring.

And she smelled better. Luc appreciated the fact that he didn't have to keep fighting the allure of her blood. As a human morsel she enticed him amply. He had needed to feed not only because he had been hungry, but because when he was hungry, resisting temptation became harder.

Now that she was cleaned up, he could see she was pretty. Her eyes had an unusual blue-gray color that reminded him of something he couldn't quite put his finger on. Her hair, wet and straight to her shoulders, showed premature streaks of white and gray amidst the dark curtain. Around her neck on a leather thong was an unusual crystal wolf's head that caught and splintered light.

A curious, unusual human to be sure. If human she was.

Luc looked at Jude, who nodded. So he began.

"I saved you," Luc said. "I took you from the park. I found you near death, and while I was preparing to take you from there, one of the rogues who attacked you arrived to finish you off. I gutted him, Dani Makar. I gutted him and broke his neck, then carried you away."

Horror and satisfaction warred on her face. Horror, no doubt, at his description of the kill, but satisfaction from knowing one of her attackers had met such a fate. She scowled. "You didn't save me for *my* sake."

"No," Luc agreed. "I brought you here for the sake of my friend, Jude. You were proof of what I had to say."

"So why should I care?"

"Because you're still alive."

Her frown deepened, but she moved uneasily. He leaned toward her, lowering his voice to that hypnotic tone that usually got vampires what they wanted. He fixed her with his gaze, holding her in thrall.

"What are you, Dani Makar?"

She didn't respond. Some mortals were immune to being vamped, although not very many, but he was disappointed anyway. They needed to know, and she was refusing to tell. He did note, however, that she didn't quite seem able to break from his gaze. At least he had that advantage.

Then he noticed something else, something that unsettled him to his very core: her gaze was holding him as much as his was holding hers. It was calling to him almost as strongly as her blood. He wanted her in every way possible.

"Merde!" he swore and tore himself away.

Chloe's sarcastic voice filled the room. "Another fail for the great St. Just."

"Chloe," Jude said sharply. "We have enough on our plates. Don't give Luc a hard time."

"At least not until you tell me I can," she said too sweetly. "Or until the next time he interferes with my life."

Luc barely spared her a glance. He was more focused on Jude, who had to make the next attempt. He noticed that Terri began to look uneasy herself, as if finally realizing that Dani might mean more trouble.

Jude spoke. He didn't even attempt to vamp Dani. "Okay. You don't want to tell us anything. But right now we're wondering if you're in league with the folks who want to start this war, because if there's one thing we all know for certain, it's that you're not purely human."

Luc switched his gaze back to Dani. She was looking at Jude now, so their gazes didn't lock. She bit her lip, clearly hesitating.

"I don't want to start, or even help in, a war among you bloodsuckers," she said finally, an edge in her voice. "I wouldn't mind if you were all dead. I want nothing to do with your kind. But I won't do a single thing that would harm a human. Not one."

"I feel enlightened," Luc said sarcastically. "While I understand your animus toward us, given what those rogues did, you still haven't answered the question. Are you a threat?"

"Not that I can do anything about it," Dani said fiercely, "but I am your mortal enemy."

She might as well have dropped a bomb in the room, she thought with satisfaction. Everyone stood perfectly still and regarded her with concern.

"Well," said Chloe, breaking the silence finally,

"I feel ever so much better. Since I'm human, I guess I can just take a hike now."

"But you won't," Terri said. A frown creased her brow. "You would harm my husband?"

"If I could," Dani said. "Husband? He holds you in thrall. You're a slave to him."

"No, I am not. He can't vamp me at all. And you don't know what you're talking about."

Jude touched her arm. "Easy, my love. She can't and won't hurt me. As long as she's not going to join the rogues, I don't care what she does."

Terri looked at him. "But we don't even know what she is."

"Dani Makar," Luc said with quiet significance.

Ice water trickled down Dani's spine, depriving her of any satisfaction she might have felt at making her opinion of vampires known.

Reluctantly, she looked at him.

"I know who you are."

He couldn't possibly know. Her heart began to gallop and her mouth turned dry. Even her family couldn't identify her as anything except a normal.

"Who?" Jude asked.

"I heard of them when I was up north. Makar. You're a member of the Makari pack, aren't you?"

His eyes bored into her. They were golden now, no longer black, but they still seemed to pin her and cleave her tongue. Deprived of speech, she could only stare.

"So, *ma belle,*" he said with soft satisfaction,

"why haven't you shifted shape? Are two of us too much?"

Her heart plummeted and her throat closed. Terror and hatred warred in her. Surely they would kill her now.

"But she doesn't smell like a lycanthrope," Jude said.

"Oh. My. God." Chloe groaned. "A werewolf? Here?"

Luc never took his gaze from her. "She's not a lycanthrope," he said. "If she were, she'd have shifted to protect herself from us. They never meet our kind in any other form."

He started smiling, and Dani wished she could spring at him like her family would and separate his head from his body. She did not like that smile at all.

"Poor, broken little wolf," he said. "You *can't* change. Did they exile you?"

Oh, how she loathed him then. But however she felt, she retained enough sense to know that springing at a vampire would only cost her, probably her life. She glared at him. "They're not like that."

He shrugged. "I really don't care. What I care about is that the mystery is solved. Now I have another question. Are you going to send for your pack? Because if you do, given the gathering of vampires that is happening right now, your pack may meet more death than success. I really wouldn't mind it, you know. The four of us can leave town."

Dani swallowed hard, torn. If this war they had

talked about really was about to happen, she certainly didn't want her pack involved. Indeed, her mother would probably shrug and say to let the vampires kill each other. On the other hand, if she didn't threaten these bloodsuckers with her pack, what might they do to her?

"If you let me go," she said finally, "I don't want to involve them."

Jude spoke. "I already told you that you could go. I don't keep prisoners." He waved to the door.

"But," said Luc softly, "it still might be wiser to wait for dawn, little wolf. Those with fewer scruples than Jude are amassing."

"Why should you care?" she demanded, struggling toward anger to banish her fear and something approaching despair. "Your kind loathes mine. You hunt us like animals."

"I thought it was the other way around," Luc said, a faint amusement in his voice. "Your kind would like to see ours exterminated. From my perspective, I have no interest in lycanthropes. They make terrible food, and if they don't attack me, then I care nothing at all one way or the other."

She didn't believe him. She'd grown up with warnings about bloodsuckers. "We don't hurt humans," she said. "You do."

"*Some* of us do," Jude said. "Which is the precise reason we're evidently about to go to war."

"Jude protects humans," Terri said, unable to conceal her anger. "Do *you?*"

Dani couldn't answer. By and large, the packs preferred to live alone and be left alone, much like ordinary wolves. They avoided mingling with humans, and they loathed vampires because they attacked humans, which no pack would do because they were human—at least part of the time. A pack killed wild game only to eat, and otherwise only in self-defense. Vampires killed for pleasure. But no, they didn't protect anything or anyone except themselves. Something like shame niggled at her, making her so uncomfortable that her anger revived.

"Why," she repeated, "do you care what happens to me?"

"Because," said Luc, "I have no quarrel with you. Unless you want to start one."

Outside in the night, sirens began to whoop. Almost at the same time, a phone tweeted.

"That's me," Terri said. "I guess I need to go to work." She rose and went to get a cell phone from the desk.

"It's your night off," Jude protested.

"If they need me, it's because it's more than the on-duty medical examiner can handle," she replied, then touched her phone and answered.

"It's begun," Luc said. "It's begun."

Jude straightened. "I'm going with her to watch over her. Chloe, you stay here no matter what. I don't want you exposed. Luc, keep an eye on both of them."

Terri disappeared into the inner sanctum and returned in a few minutes clad in jeans and a jacket. "It's going to be a long night," she remarked as she headed for the door. Jude disappeared with her.

Luc, staring at the two women, sighed. *"C'est la guerre."*

Chloe sat working at her desk. Luc appeared lost in somber thought. Dani was left to dart looks at them between staring down at her hands, which clenched and unclenched as emotions roiled through her like racing white water.

The vampires were going to war. For her kind that ought to be cause for jubilation, except she knew who would get caught in the middle: humans. While she was not fully human herself, she was human enough. She had lived among humans long enough to be horrified at that and ashamed that her own pack would probably stand aside and let it happen.

Lycanthropes didn't involve themselves in the affairs of humans or nonhumans if they could avoid it. They preferred a solitary existence among their own kind, to live free and to be safe. Their lives were, for the most part, contented if not always happy. Their own little world.

But tonight had altered her view. Just a little. It didn't feel like an earthquake yet, but some inner voice warned her that it could become one.

She looked up again and found Chloe studying her.

Chloe spoke. "So you're a werewolf?"

"Not really." Her shame, her sorrow, but true.

"You can't shape-shift?"

"No."

Chloe shook her head. "Well, I'm glad you can't. But *you* probably aren't."

"I hate it."

"I guess I would, too, if I were you. But you weren't exiled?"

"No." Dani didn't want to talk about it. Didn't want to touch on the grief and longing that had made her leave of her own accord to try to live life as a normal. She ached to run with her pack, yet she couldn't. She couldn't live with the daily reminder that she was different, or with the feeling that she was a burden and not an equal. No one had encouraged her to leave, not a single one. She simply couldn't take being the only normal in the pack.

Much as she disliked Luc, she couldn't deny she was exactly what he had called her: a broken wolf.

She sighed and looked at the clock, counting the hours until dawn. Since it was winter, dawn remained far away.

"So you live here now?" Chloe asked. "What do you do?"

"I work in university administration and take classes when I can."

"What kind of classes?"

Considering the horror Chloe had initially expressed over Dani's lycanthropy, her questions now seemed surprisingly friendly. "Whatever I need. I'm just starting, but I think I'd like to be a nurse."

Luc made a sound and she reluctantly looked at him.

"Another altruist."

"What's wrong with that?" she demanded.

"I don't recall saying anything was wrong with it," he retorted.

"Your tone."

"A thousand pardons, *ma chère dame.*"

"Don't mind him," Chloe said. "He's always a pain. Between being a former French aristocrat and losing his mate last year, he's a little insane. We make excuses for him."

Luc barely blinked, but to Dani he seemed to tense. Dani didn't think poking a vampire was exactly smart, but Chloe apparently thought she was perfectly safe.

More food for thought, thoughts that crashed hard against her belief that all vampires were bloodsucking monsters.

"What *were* you, Luc?" Chloe asked. "A duke or something?"

Luc waved a hand and for a few seconds it appeared he wouldn't answer. "You are full of questions, Chloe."

"I'm curious, since I'm stuck with you."

"I was the Marquis de St. Just."

"A real honest-to-gosh marquis." Chloe's voice dripped sarcasm. "I'm impressed."

"Don't be, *ma petite.* All it brought me was a dank prison cell and the promise of a ride on the tumbrel to the guillotine."

Astonishment filled Dani. He was that old? But Chloe had a different reaction, and dropped her sarcasm entirely.

"Is that why you became a vampire?"

"It was the only way to survive. Enough. I don't care to discuss my past, *s'il vous plaît.*"

Chloe put her chin in her hand. "It's going to be a long night if both of you keep imitating clams."

Surprisingly, Dani felt a little bubble of laughter rising. She tried to quell it but failed, and a giggle escaped her. A reaction to all the stress of the night, she thought, but Chloe was certainly a piece of work.

Chloe grinned at her. "Neither of you exactly looks like a clam." She paused. "Here's the thing. I know something about vampires, having worked for Jude for years. But I really don't know anything about werewolves, and I'm curious. As for you, Luc, a little illumination would go a long way. You owe me for having kidnapped me."

"As I recall, that was one of my stupider moments and you made me regret my idiocy almost from the first second."

"He kidnapped you," Dani said, aghast.

"For all of ten minutes," Chloe admitted. "He needed an entrée with a friend of Jude's and he'd already ticked the guy off. So I was his key." She shrugged. "I was mad at the time because once he carried me off to Creed's, I didn't have my car. I had to wait *hours* to catch the bus."

Dani listened in astonishment. What upset Chloe was waiting to take the bus? Not being kidnapped?

"Of course, I didn't like being kidnapped for general reasons. Like not having a say about where I was going or when." She frowned at Luc.

"I apologized. Would you like another one?"

Chloe waved her hand. "I doubt it would be sincere now." She sighed, then looked at the clock herself. "Just tell me, St. Just. How bad could it get?"

"You saw the condition Dani was in. Multiply that by dozens a night. All of it to force a confrontation with Jude. They plan a reign of terror, because that is what they will enjoy. Jude is just an excuse for it."

Chloe's frown looked frightened. "Will others come to help him?"

"I don't know. Creed perhaps."

"But he can't stand against a whole bunch of vampires. Not alone."

"I did not say he would be alone. But how many come to help and when, I cannot say. The minute these vampires begin their spree, this city will become unsafe for both our kinds. Some may choose to wait for another time and place to rid us of these rogues. I simply don't know."

"Couldn't Jude just leave? Why don't they just come here and confront him?"

"I told you, they want their amusement. And they

know Jude well enough. He won't leave because he won't want a single human to suffer because of him. If he turned his back on this city, they might still do as they plan, and possibly more of it. This is a start, Chloe. These rogues want to satisfy their lusts unfettered. So far they have never gotten together in a large group, and thus we have been able to control them. It was always one or two at a time, and if they would not agree to follow the rule, then we would get rid of them."

He closed his eyes a moment. "There are places where *they* rule. Few and far between, but not places I would choose to dwell. Not all the monster stories you hear are folklore and legend."

"I kind of figured that out when I met *you.*"

Luc didn't respond to the insult. "You see," he said quietly, "as technology and communications improve, they must hide farther and farther away, going to places where the people are regarded as so primitive that no one believes the stories. Places where deaths and maulings can be blamed on other animals. But now they want a modern city."

"They won't succeed."

His eyes snapped open. "Tell me, Chloe, how the news will report tonight's murders tomorrow night. They will at first assume there is a madman. As the killings mount, they will consider a gang of some sort. How long do you think it will be before any humans start speaking openly of vampires? But Jude will know. And Jude will try to stop them. That's what they want. And once they've removed Jude, they can hold the city in thrall with terror and take their victims by will. Because so few of you can resist our enticements. You are drawn to us, you obey us, you want us."

Chloe looked glum. Dani felt again that icy trickle along her spine. The image he painted revolted and terrified her.

"Merde!" He rose to his feet and started pacing, moving so quickly he was almost impossible to see.

"Quit it," Chloe said. "You're making me dizzy."

"Then close your eyes." But he slowed down.

"What about you?" Chloe asked. "Are you going to help Jude?"

"Right now I am finding it difficult to be in this room. I am the fox guarding the henhouse."

Dani drew her legs beneath her, ready to leap from the couch. "Can you control yourself, fox?"

Swiftly he crossed to her and bent over her. He closed his golden eyes and drew a deep breath. She knew he was smelling her. Helplessly, she shrank back.

"You smell like a banquet," he said. "You arouse my hunger, even though I'm not hungry. Take heed."

Then, before she knew he had moved, he was back in his chair. "Yes," he said flatly, "I can control myself. But it does not make me less dangerous."

That was a mixed-up statement, she thought as

she started breathing again. He could control himself but he was still dangerous?

She fell silent, thinking that never before had she felt so caught between the devil and the deep blue sea.

Chapter 3

Luc St. Just had grown used to loathing himself. He'd certainly done enough of it since Natasha's passing. But now he almost revolted himself because the little wolf not only roused his hunger, but she awoke his sexual desires, as well.

He didn't want to desire anyone ever again. And he certainly didn't want to desire a mutant lycanthrope. While he said he didn't care one way or another about them, the truth was the whole notion of shape-shifting disturbed him. He might be an abomination but at least he was the same thing *all* the time. Besides, whatever form they took, they were still dogs. Something atavistic in him rebelled at being attracted to one.

Trouble was, she smelled human. She *did* smell

like a banquet to him, a banquet he too often denied himself since Natasha because he had refused to become intimate with anyone ever again.

But this woman had awakened nearly somnolent urges in him. He couldn't quite ignore the way his pulse accelerated, the way she called to his hunger, the way she made him want to act like one of those rogues out there.

Well, not like one of them, certainly. No, he would woo and seduce her, and teach her delights unlike any she had ever imagined.

And her eyes… Those blue-gray eyes of hers were hypnotic. He wanted to keep looking into them, yet feared their call.

It would be so easy to give in. All that held him back was Chloe's presence and Jude's admonition. Otherwise he would reach for her, touch her, taste her, and by the time he was done, she would no longer think vampires were monsters. Oh, no.

He caught himself, reminding himself of his promises not to get involved again, however briefly. Then it struck him that the way she called to him gave her more power than it gave him.

The irony was not lost on him.

But it also gave him a jolt. Not once in over two hundred years had he ever considered that his desires could enslave him. Yet here he was, with a powerful thirst for a female, one that was in danger of overcoming his sense.

The hunger was part of him, deep, persuasive,

pervasive, unlike any hunger or want he had known as a human. During the Reign of Terror, when he had been changed, he had been like most new vampires: famished and out of control. Only, in his case, surrounded by so much bloodshed, no one had tried to stop him.

But eventually calm had returned to the world, and with it a need for caution. One night he had arisen from the sleep of death to realize that if he didn't want to be forever on the move every few days or weeks, he needed to find a better way.

As a result he had lived successfully in Paris for at least half his life, alternating every decade or so with some other city.

But now he realized something else. Jude's determination to enforce the rule had another purpose than protecting vampires from discovery or humans from predation. It also ensured that a vampire was not a slave to his innate needs.

That modicum of self-restraint was all that separated a vampire from becoming a true monster. It provided their only claim to being truly civilized.

Luc had always held himself to be utterly civilized. It disturbed him to think he might not be even yet.

He forced himself to look at Dani while quashing his own urges. What he saw was a frightened young woman who had been through hell tonight. Considering the attack she had suffered, it was amazing she wasn't falling to pieces.

But then the hunger rose again and he had to look away. Chloe, surprisingly, didn't tempt him at all.

What was going on? In the past all humans had struck him as equally edible. It was, after all, only their blood he wanted, and very little of it, actually. Some were certainly more attractive than others and made better playmates, but this response was different.

He didn't like it.

He desperately wanted to walk away now, to escape from the enticing scent that filled this room, but he couldn't. Jude's office provided a likely target if the rogues decided on a frontal assault.

Some remnant of honor and integrity held him rooted.

Just then, reaction hit Dani. The air was suddenly tinged with terror—another enticing scent to his kind—and he looked at her. She had begun to shake, and her eyes were almost wild.

"Chloe," he said. "Get a blanket or something. She's feeling the shock."

Chloe leaped up and headed to a small room. When she opened the door he could see a bed and some other creature comforts. She returned swiftly with a thick down-filled duvet and draped it over Dani.

"You're safe now," Chloe murmured. "It's all over."

Perhaps, but she hadn't processed it yet. Luc

watched as her head swiveled, then shook back and forth as if she were denying something.

"I can't...I can't breathe."

"Yes, you can," Luc said. "Force yourself. Deep, slow breaths."

Dani tried, and after a few minutes her breathing achieved a more normal pattern. Then tears rolled down her cheeks.

"Do you know what they did to me?" she said. "Do you have any idea what it was like to be attacked that way? There were four of them. *Four.* I couldn't fight them off. Why would they do that to anyone?"

"Because they're sick and twisted," Chloe answered sharply. "Reason enough. At least you survived. An ordinary human would have died."

Dani didn't seem to hear. "They were so strong. How could anything be that strong? They didn't need four of them. One could have done it. But they all took part and laughed."

Luc swore and sprang to his feet. He began to pace at a furious speed, not caring if he made Chloe dizzy, or if they couldn't see him at all. He tried to exist above it all, but the simple fact was sometimes his own kind sickened him. Some vestige of his human existence, he supposed.

Regardless, right now he wanted to rip the heads off a few vampires.

He stopped pacing and looked at her. "Did you

hear any names? See anything that would help me identify them?"

"I don't think so. Why?"

"Because I'd like to visit the wrath of hell on them."

Her eyes widened again, and he could see she didn't doubt him one bit.

"There are four of them," she whispered.

"Three now, remember. I executed one of them when he came back for you, and frankly, I would like to do the same to all the rest. If you remember anything, tell me." It was not a request.

She gave a tiny nod. He could see the shock on her face, her difficulty in believing he had killed one of his own kind to protect her. Of course she would find that hard to believe.

"I saw what they did to you," he said. "I saw it when I found you. I know what they are and they deserve punishment. I'd have hunted them then, but I couldn't leave you. So I will hunt them tomorrow night. Or the next night. But I will hunt them and find them."

A little shudder passed through her.

"That's what they intend for others in this city," Luc went on. "It cannot be allowed."

"My, my," said Chloe. "Luc the Avenger. Who would have thought?"

"You don't know me," he said shortly.

He wasn't sure he knew himself anymore. Since Natasha's death he had changed, and now it was as if a veil lifted and he truly saw what he had become. Jude was right: he was wallowing.

How revolting.

He sank back into the chair, although he felt like going out to run as fast as the wind, climb walls and execute vampires. He could barely restrain himself.

But restraint was essential, he reminded himself. Restraint because he had to guard these women, restraint because if he let his self-control crack even one bit he might do exactly the wrong thing, like pounce on Dani.

God, why did she call to him so?

Chloe sat beside her, rubbing her shoulder, passing her tissues, occasionally hugging her while she cried.

There was a time he would have done that, but not since his change. Now it was too dangerous.

Just what the devil had he become in order to save himself from the guillotine?

Dani calmed down eventually. Crying had exhausted her. But the earthquake she had sensed in the offing had arrived.

She was afraid. How could she look at a vampire as a savior? But she did, and it filled her with fear.

She'd never been afraid like this in her life. Her pack had always protected her. Now she was alone—like most humans, she admitted—and she had fears such as she had never known before. Fear of the night. Fear of being attacked. Fear that her life could be ripped from her by these rogues gearing up for war.

War against a single vampire. Four of them had attacked her, and however strong vampires might be, she was quite certain that one couldn't stand against three or possibly more. Maybe Luc would help them, but even then the odds didn't look good.

She reminded herself that she wasn't really involved. She'd just been in the wrong place at the wrong time. It might have happened to anyone who had been in the park at that time. Apparently from the way Terri had hurried out, it may have happened to any number of others already.

But the earth-shattering thing was that it had happened to *her*. What's more, now that she understood what was going on, she knew that it could happen again.

Maybe she should catch the first morning bus home and just get out of here. Go back to the safety of the pack.

But then another thought occurred to her. Would her pack even be safe if the rogue vampires took over? It didn't look like an immediate threat, but somewhere in the future it could become one. Because despite Luc's announced indifference to her kind, she knew all vampires didn't feel the same.

Her kind? Oh, God, she wasn't her pack's kind. That much was obvious. She belonged nowhere at all.

Finally she looked at Chloe and admitted the most obvious thing. "I'm afraid to go home now."

"You're safe in the daylight."

"I know. But what about when it becomes dark again?"

Chloe said nothing.

"Here is not a safe place," Luc said heavily. "As well guarded as Jude keeps it, it's not totally impermeable to vampires. Little is."

"The protection was mainly designed to keep humans out while he sleeps," Chloe said.

"Exactly."

Chloe looked at Dani. "What are we going to do for you?"

"Most especially if they somehow find out that she survived the attack."

Dani's mouth dried. Her palms grew damp and she wiped them on the too-tight borrowed jeans. "How would they learn that?"

Luc shrugged. "Perhaps they will find the one I killed before dawn removes his carcass. Perhaps because your body is gone? Because you are not listed among the victims of tonight's mayhem in tomorrow night's news?"

"Why would they care?"

"The entire point of this little war they want to start is that none of them likes to be thwarted."

Dani's heart skipped at least two beats, then settled into an edgy rhythm. From the way Luc's eyes narrowed, she suspected he could hear it. Hell, he could probably smell the fear clinging to her. *She* would have been able to had it not been her own.

"You're getting a lot of shocks tonight, aren't you?" Chloe said. "First the attack, then being rescued by a vampire and learning that not all of them are vicious killers. Well, it would set anyone back on their heels. And I'm afraid, too, though not as afraid as you because I haven't been attacked."

"We need to find a safe place for her," Luc said. "Daylight hours take care of themselves, but then there's the rest of the time."

"I often leave work after dark," Dani said. Because it was winter, she now left her office at dusk or later. Even thinking about stepping out into the night made her mouth go dry now.

"Then we have to find a way to protect you."

"We?" Chloe said. "When did you become we?"

"I think I have joined the fight."

"Oh, great. Can you promise not to go haywire again?"

"Most certainly." His eyes narrowed and a faint smile came to his mouth. And all of a sudden he appeared more attractive than Dani would have believed possible. His blond hair gleamed, his face relaxed, and she wished he were not a vampire. "I think," he said, "that I have found reason to live again."

"Great," Chloe said. "I'm sure the world will rejoice. And I just love those odds. Two vampires against a horde."

Dani giggled again, maybe because she was nervous. "It *does* sound like the Alamo."

"Perhaps," Luc agreed. "But sometimes we have no choice. They will be maddened by their blood lust. So, it seems, we will be smarter, yes?" His gaze settled on Dani. "But first we must protect our little wolf."

"Please don't call me that."

Luc's brow lifted. "Why not?"

"Because I'm not…because I can't…" She looked down and covered her face with a corner of the comforter.

"Je suis désolé," Luc said, actually sounding sincere. "I'm sorry. I did not know I touched on a nerve."

Chloe spoke. "So you didn't leave entirely of your own volition?"

Dani's head shot up and she looked at Chloe. "I did. It was *my* choice. I didn't fit and I couldn't stand it anymore."

"I know that feeling well," Luc said quietly. "All too well."

Dani searched his face and for the first time in her life it occurred to her that bloodsuckers might have real feelings beyond satisfying their blood lusts. That they might actually think and feel like the humans they had once been. Some of them, anyway.

She told herself she didn't want his sympathy, certainly not the sympathy of one of his kind. Yet her throat tightened, anyway. She had no one anymore, no one. She had left her family behind and had barely started to make friends. Certainly not friends with whom she could trust her true story. So she skimmed the surface, pretending to be just like everyone else when she was not.

Now her story had come out in the unlikeliest company possible, and she found sympathy in the gaze of one her pack would call their mortal enemy.

How was she supposed to deal with this?

From earliest childhood she had been taught to use her nose above every other sense. She had been trained to identify things as good or bad by those scents, and the scent of vampire had been drilled into her as a threat. Even a whiff of it could cause her to shudder.

Tonight she had been attacked by bloodsuckers, their stench overpowering. Because she could not change, she hadn't been able to outrun them or fight them off.

But now she had to deal with the fact that one of that kind had saved her, and another was keeping her safe in his office…and the smell was all around her, and it was not bad.

Linked to terrors she had been taught, but not at all repugnant in and of itself. Separated from her childhood training, the smell was actually pleasant. Even enticing.

Perhaps that was why she had been trained to avoid it. Because it might draw her in. By itself, there was nothing to cause repulsion.

God, she felt like she was losing her mind. The echoes of the attack still reverberated through her, and yet she was drawn to one of their kind. But that was how they operated, she reminded herself. Not by repelling, but by attracting. Like spiders weaving sparkling webs that looked like a safe place to land.

However alluring, there was nothing safe about a vampire. Hadn't Luc said so himself?

Chloe excused herself to go make tea. She disappeared around a corner, and soon there were sounds of cupboards opening and closing, of water running.

Luc spoke, his voice pitched low. "Your eyes reveal too much, Dani Makar. As do your scents. You want me and you do not like it."

She drew a shocked breath, horrified that he could tell so much.

He gave her a half smile. "You have few secrets when it comes to your feelings. I can smell them. Too bad you cannot smell mine."

Her voice came out a broken whisper. "Why?"

"Because then you would know I want you, too."

She couldn't breathe. Her heart hammered so loudly it filled her ears. "I don't..."

He shrugged. "It makes no difference. I have no interest in my wants or yours. Mine can be satisfied elsewhere, and yours...well, your reluctance hardly appeals to me."

"I thought your kind liked that."

"Some do. They are the ones we will have to fight. It's never been much to my taste."

She felt he was omitting information, but she was fairly certain she didn't want to know what it was.

Bad enough he'd been so blunt and exposed something she had scarcely faced herself. She had the worst urge to slap him or storm out, but knew she couldn't do either.

She was trapped until dawn with a vampire who perceived too much, and feelings she hoped she would eventually be able to forget ever having. Her family would be so ashamed of her.

She swallowed hard and was so glad when Chloe returned with two mugs of hot tea. It gave her something to hold and something to do. The need to stay active grew stronger with each passing minute. The problem was she couldn't imagine what she could do. She had no way to pursue her attackers. She couldn't bring this to the police, who wouldn't believe any of it, and she couldn't fight a bunch of vampires, anyway.

Unless she made what her family would consider an unholy alliance.

But her attraction to Luc terrified her. Now that she'd been forced to face it, she wanted to find a hole to bury it in. It would have been nice to blame it on the shock of the attack she had experienced earlier, but she was quite certain that wasn't it. Based on the attack, all she should be feeling was horror and repulsion.

She felt as if her beliefs and her feelings had been tossed into a cement mixer. The pattern of her own thoughts and reactions felt alien, as if they belonged to someone else. She needed solitude to sort herself out again, to settle all these shocks. But she would have none until dawn.

Luc spoke. "We should send you back to your family first thing tomorrow. Away from here, away from all danger."

She had been trying to build a life, to escape depending on her family. To leave behind the constant yearning that gnawed at her, the yearning to be fully one of her pack. To go back before she had achieved her full independence and grown the confidence she had come here to find seemed like failure. Utter failure.

She was always failing. Did she want to again?

But when she allowed her mind to touch on the attack, she wondered if failure wouldn't be better. If Luc was right, that those rogues would know she hadn't died and that this was all about hating to be thwarted, she would certainly be on their list for coming nights.

She couldn't stand against them alone. If she ran, she'd fail. If she stayed, she might die.

But somehow that last thought crystallized something in her.

Better to die than live a life of fear and self-loathing. She wouldn't go back to her pack with her tail between her legs—even if she didn't have a tail.

No.

Worse, if she told them what had happened to her to send her home, they might feel obligated to come down here and hunt for vengeance. Oh, there was no *might* about it. They would come.

"I can't go home," she announced. "I can't. If my pack finds out what happened they'll come here to avenge me. I don't want them in the middle of your war."

Luc nodded then sighed. "I doubt they would discriminate between the rogues who attacked you and the rest of us."

"No, they wouldn't."

"Then it's best not to let them know. Things will be difficult enough without a pack of angry wolves getting into it."

"So what do we do with her?" Chloe demanded. "Cripes, Luc, you're full of problems and don't have any solutions."

"Oh, I have a solution," Luc said almost bitterly. "I'll protect her. I can spirit her away if I sense a threat." Then he looked at Dani. "If she will let me, of course."

Dani's heart sank. She wanted most of all to get away from this damnably attractive bloodsucker who was making her feel things she didn't want, making her want things that ought to make her shudder. Just looking at him sent a shiver of desire through her. The vampire magnetism, she told herself. That's all it was. Hadn't her family warned her?

Her reply, when it came, was heavy with dislike. "What choice do I have?"

"None, *ma petite,*" he said. "None. These rogues

have narrowed the choices for all of us. They will get their war. And they will not succeed."

"So sure?" Chloe asked acidly.

"No. But it never pays to go into battle full of doubt."

With that, he appeared to draw into himself, to ponder whatever unhappy thoughts darkened his face.

Jude returned in the hour before dawn. His first words were "It's begun. Four violent murders tonight."

"Terri?" Chloe asked with instant concern.

"She's at the morgue surrounded by enough people to be safe. Whoever the rogues are, they weren't interested in following the bodies. And soon they'll be going to ground."

"Did you learn anything else?" Luc asked.

"Other than that the bodies reeked of vampire? No. From time to time while I was watching Terri on the streets, I thought I caught a whiff of them, but they seemed to have kept moving all night."

"So they do not yet feel truly confident," Luc remarked.

"That would be my guess. It may be that so far there are only those that attacked Dani."

Luc waved a hand. "Perhaps. If they can't gather others to their cause, they can deal with that quickly enough. Perhaps tomorrow night we'll have fewer bodies. And the next night we'll be dealing with newborns."

Chloe gasped. Dani asked, "Newborns?"

Luc's golden gaze had darkened a bit. "Newborns," he repeated. "The newly changed. The most dangerous vampires of all."

Apprehension prickled through Dani. "Why?"

"Because they're the strongest vampires of all. Because they're voracious and out of control. The last time I had to deal with a new vampire, it terrorized an entire city and it took two of us to execute it."

Dani drew a long, shaky breath.

"You see," Luc continued, "those are the stories which persuade your kind to see my kind as such a threat. Most of the undead follow certain rules. The newborns follow no rules at all."

Chloe slumped at her desk. "No wonder you don't want to change Terri."

Jude spoke. "It's possible to prepare someone for the change and make it easier by providing plenty of food. But if you leave them on their own, yes, that's where you get true monsters. What a devil of a thought, Luc."

"I'm trying to think of everything. How else can we prepare?"

"Damned if I know," Jude said almost wearily. "All right. Time is short right now. You need a place to go to ground, Luc. Soon. And then it'll be safe for

Dani and Chloe to go home. That leaves darkfall to deal with."

"I'm not leaving this office, boss," Chloe said firmly. "I'll sleep right here." Then she looked at Dani. "Can you get home by yourself once it's light?"

"Of course." She sounded more certain than she felt, though. Yesterday she had felt completely safe in this city, and now she didn't feel safe at all. Not even knowing the bloodsuckers couldn't roam in the daylight eased her apprehension.

Chloe hesitated. "I'll drive you home at dawn. Then I'm coming back here to get ready for the siege."

Chapter 4

Luc waited for Dani outside the university building where she worked. Chloe had managed to get the information from her, and while he didn't exactly want to be here, he knew no one else could promise Dani any kind of safety.

He smelled the approach of snow on the air and suspected that before the night was over, a white blanket would cover the city. It mattered to him not one way or the other, for he felt neither cold nor heat, but it might slow the rogues down a bit. It would be hard for them not to leave trails that even human eyes could read once it snowed.

He had donned clothing unfamiliar to him: a parka, rather than the leather that he preferred because it could stand up to the treatment he gave it, and jeans—the human preference for which he could not begin to understand. He hoped to blend in as he stood here waiting.

Already the city was on heightened alert because of the four murders last night, all of them grotesque, savage enough to hide any evidence vampires were involved. He didn't want to appear out of place at all. Not now, not when he was here to protect Dani. Another time it would have made no difference to him, but tonight he could not take to the rooftops or vanish swiftly and without warning, not unless he wanted to terrorize Dani more than she already had been.

He saw her emerge from the building, wrapped in a long coat with a knit scarf around her neck and a knit cap on her unusual hair.

He forced himself to walk at a human pace toward her.

"Good evening," he called, so his appearance wouldn't startle her.

She turned to look at him, and those amazing eyes of hers widened then narrowed. "Chloe told you," she said.

"But of course. I said I would protect you."

She looked as if she desperately wanted to argue but thought better of it. She glanced around at the darkness held at bay only by the walkway lamps around the campus and then back at him. Truly a choice of evils. The thought amused him.

"We will walk," he said and stepped toward her,

offering his arm. It was an old habit, but he wasn't at all surprised when she visibly hesitated. Finally she took his arm reluctantly.

"We can take the campus bus."

"Perhaps you can. I cannot."

"Why not?"

"How much torture do you expect me to subject myself to?"

"Torture? Oh."

He watched the understanding dawn on her face and enjoyed it. Damned if he was going to pretend to be something other than what he was. As Chloe would have said, she could "like it or lump it."

Then she startled him by asking, "What do you live for?"

It had been a very long time since a question had set him back on his heels. They continued to wend their way through the campus, heading toward public streets that he knew to be lined with apartments frequented by students.

Prime hunting ground, because youth made many students relatively fearless, and they came and went at all hours of the night to visit one another or get something to eat.

"What do I live for?" he repeated, even as he began scoping the vicinity with an eye to see how easy or difficult it would be to hunt. "Why should you care?"

"I don't know," she admitted.

"What do *you* live for?"

Satisfaction filled him when she didn't answer. It wasn't a question easily answered by anyone, and certainly it was not the kind he cared to discuss with a virtual stranger. Even a stranger who smelled like ambrosia and awakened his every instinct to take her, drink from her and come to know her in that intimate, exquisite place only vampires and their lovers could go.

They reached her street eventually and he paused, surveying everything intently.

"Do you smell something?" she asked.

"City smells, humans. Coming snow."

"Then why do you look so concerned?"

"Because this would be a marvelous place to hunt."

She stiffened, but she didn't pull away. "How so?"

He raised his other arm and began pointing. "See all the dark places between the buildings? All the large evergreen shrubs? The little alcoves around doorways, not all of which are lit?"

"Yes…"

"Those rogues would look at this place as a smorgasbord."

"Oh, no," she whispered.

"You have reason for concern."

"Yes, but I'm not just worried about myself. Most of the people living here are just kids."

"I know. All the more tempting." He shook his head. "I will keep my assessments to myself, if that will make you more comfortable. But I must say, if this is where you live, I am reluctant to leave you alone here."

"I can lock myself in."

"Locks don't stop us if we choose to ignore them."

He felt the shudder pass through her and smelled her rising level of fear. That scent called to his kind and inevitably would call to the others.

"You're practically a beacon," he said irritably. "Your fear is perfuming the air. Let's get to your place before we discuss what to do to protect you."

She didn't argue. Indeed, she quickened her step, guiding him toward her apartment on the third floor. The alcove around her door was lit, but it didn't reassure him.

He stayed her hand as she started to use her key, holding it back until he had inhaled the air around the edges of her door.

"It's empty," he said finally and let her open the door.

She stepped quickly within, closing the door behind them and locking it before she even turned on a light.

What Luc saw affected him. She owned little, and what she owned appeared to be very much second- or thirdhand. Little spots of color, like a pillow here and there, and the dishes on her counter tried to liven the tiny space. Not that *he* owned much anymore. Not since Natasha. He had plenty of money, just no desire to spend it. He suspected this was a very different situation.

She hurried over to her kitchenette, as if she wanted to put distance between them, and began a pot of coffee. Then she pulled something from the freezer and put it into a small microwave.

He took the opportunity to check out her apartment, including the bedroom behind the closed door. The quality of construction was about as poor as the builders could get away with, and even the walls looked worn from abuse.

He returned to find her waiting, watching. Uneasiness roiled in her. She didn't like having him here, but he suspected she would like being alone even less.

"Eat," he said as the microwave pinged. "While you do, we'll discuss measures to protect you."

She nodded slowly, then turned to pull a prepackaged dinner out of the microwave. A cup of coffee soon sat beside it on the tiny dinette. He settled onto one of the creaky chairs facing her.

"This apartment affords little protection," he told her flatly. "If you insist on staying here, you must keep your windows and doors tightly closed at night."

"I'm not sure I'll ever go out at night again."

"It must feel that way right now. But trust me, Dani, you would not like to live as I do, claiming only half the day for yourself. When we have taken care of this problem, you'll learn to feel safe again."

"Maybe."

His gaze fixed on her lips as she licked away a

bit of food. Her mouth had a lovely shape, and the plumpness of her lips enticed him. His entire body responded with a hunger so intense he froze for a few seconds, fighting it, seeking self-control. It wasn't easy.

"Do you have a home?" she asked.

He froze. Memories threatened to spill over the dam he had constructed. *Natasha!* But no, he could not allow that now. "What do you mean by 'home'? I consider Paris my home. Do you mean where do I live?"

"Where do you live? I mean, you must need a special sort of place during the daytime. Do you have a place that's yours here in town?"

He shook his head. "I make do. One can always find a place dark enough, especially in a city like this."

"So the rogues have no trouble, either."

"No. But if it snows, they'll have a new set of problems to deal with."

"Why?"

"Because not even a vampire can fail to leave tracks in the snow. The question is whether they'll care."

"Why do you say that?"

"Because if they cared about those things, they wouldn't be starting this fight."

She ate another few mouthfuls before speaking again. He tried not to watch.

"So they don't care if they're discovered?"

"The night is safe for them because they're awake and they have numbers. No vampire can threaten them in the daylight, and they don't really fear humans." He paused as a thought struck him. "They clearly don't want secrecy. They want to emerge from the shadows and achieve reality."

"But they *are* real."

"Of course. But living life as a legend that not even their prey believe in…well, that's a form of unreality." He paused again, thinking it through. "They're tired of being fairy tales. Humans love a good vampire book or movie, but they don't walk the streets afraid that one will leap out at them. They don't accord us any respect." He nodded slowly. "Yes, that's part of it, I'm sure. They want to be known, to be real and to exercise their power. They want to gain respect through terror."

Dani put her fork down and pushed her meal away. "That's horrible. I can't even imagine wanting that. My pack…we prefer that no one is aware of us at all. We like the anonymity, the freedom to just be what we are. We avoid humans and vampires and other things that aren't like us."

"You can make that choice. Unfortunately, the survival of my kind is intimately tied to the humans on this planet."

"You couldn't drink the blood of something else?"

"Not indefinitely."

She looked down and absently stirred her coffee.

"What would these rogues do, if they killed off everyone?"

"Oh, they won't kill everyone. They know better. I'm sure they'd find enough humans they could turn into slaves."

Dani shook her head and now pushed her coffee away. "That can't happen."

"It could, but we need to ensure it doesn't. But the important thing right now is that we find a way to make you safe. If I'm with you every minute of the night, I'll be no help to Jude. If I'm not with you, you might fall into danger again."

He rose from the table, desperately needing to put space between them. The pulse in her throat, her scent, her lips, her eyes...everything about her woke his most primal needs and desires. Much as she despised vampires, she had no idea of the pleasures he could show her, the absolute heaven that lay between life and death.

But he knew, and it made him both restless and dangerous. The need for action filled him, the only antidote to desire.

The room was too small to truly escape. Worse, he could smell moments of desire passing through her, too. They came and went like waves on a shore, as she battled them down. What was it about her? Since Natasha he'd never felt anything like this, nor did he want to.

Maybe he was just emerging at last from the claiming. Maybe he was feeling what he had felt in the days before Natasha, and he just couldn't remember it.

He turned his back to Dani and reached for the cell phone Jude had given him. Jude gave them to everyone he worked with so they could be instantly in touch. More like a radio, he supposed, than a phone. Not that he paid a whole lot of attention to most modern technologies. He had no use for most of them.

But this one was about to prove convenient. Jude answered immediately.

"We need a better place for Dani to stay. Her apartment affords little more protection than a cardboard box, and the neighborhood is perfect for hunting."

He heard Dani's gasp, but ignored it as he listened to Jude. When he finished, he turned to her.

"I'm taking you to Jude's office. Bundle up and pack a bag. It's going to be cold at the speeds I'll use."

"Now wait one minute," she said, though her eyes looked more worried than angry. "I have a life. I have things I need to do."

"That's just it, *mon trésor.* You have a life. We'd all like for you to keep it. Jude is going to locate a safe place for you to stay. In the meantime, I want you out of here."

"But why?"

"Because if anyone, *anyone,* we can't trust has found out what happened last night and that you survived, they're going to want to finish it. Not even I can protect you against three of them." He paused then added, "I may even have increased your danger."

She gasped. "How?"

"By killing that one that came back for you. They know he's missing. What if he told them he was going to finish you? If they went looking for him, they will know you were gone, too."

For a few seemingly endless minutes, she didn't move. He watched emotions play over her face, but couldn't read them all, either by sight or scent. It had been a long time since he had tried to read a human in more than the most basic ways.

Whatever she was thinking, she made up her mind. "All right," she said quietly. "But I want to make one thing perfectly clear."

"Yes?"

"If I can't escape this fight, then I want to be part of it."

"But why?"

"Because these rogues must be stopped."

She rose and went to pack, leaving him to wonder what she hadn't said. No one in their right mind would want to get into the middle of this fight if they could avoid it.

That meant something else was pushing her and that could be cause for serious concern.

The little home she'd made for herself wasn't much, but Dani resented having to leave it behind with no idea when she'd return, if ever. Even less did she like having a bloodsucker take charge.

But not even a certain innate stubbornness, the stubbornness that had caused her to leave her pack despite their objections and strike out on her own, could outweigh common sense. Maybe a few days ago it would have been different. But not after being attacked.

As she jammed items into a duffel, enough to get by for at least a few days, she thought about irony. Life, she decided, was ultimately ironic. To depend for survival on the very beings she had been taught to abhor was irony enough for an entire lifetime. Finding herself incredibly attracted to one reached even beyond that.

She paused in her packing and closed her eyes. Luc St. Just was right behind her eyelids, waiting for her. Just thinking about him made her throb deep inside, a feeling she wasn't very familiar with. She'd been battling it since last night, and rather than easing, her attraction to him seemed to be growing.

Not good. Damn, her pack would disown her.

That thought should have pulled her up short, but it didn't succeed. Instead, she continued to feel the simmering, unwanted yearning he had awakened in her.

And she couldn't even figure out what caused it. He wasn't the most likable guy in the world. He hadn't attempted to do even one thing to make her like him.

Yet there he was waiting for her in her living room, promising protection she loathed having to need, and he just wouldn't go away.

But did she want him to go away? That question really disturbed her. She shouldn't even be asking it.

Her body seemed to have developed a mind of its own, one that yielded to no logic or reason. It insisted on feeling an almost smoky desire, something intangible that wound thickly around her and made her pulse leap when he was near.

"Damn," she whispered and resumed packing. "Double damn."

Taking her cue from him, she changed from her work clothes into jeans and a sweater and boots. Then she pulled out a parka she had recently bought but had only needed a few times here so far.

That parka struck her as a reminder of her difference. Her pack dealt with the cold by changing or by wearing wolfskin clothing. She had left her own skin and fur clothing behind because it would have aroused comment. But each time she put this new parka on, it reminded her that something was wrong with her. With each rustle of the nylon, she hated it.

When she was ready, Luc shouldered her bag and they left the building together. Once they were on the street, she noted the way his gaze kept searching every nook and cranny around them, the way he tested the air repeatedly.

Then he said, "You're going to have to get on my back now."

"What?"

"I smell another vampire, and I don't recognize the scent. See those deep shadows over there? We're going to walk to them and then I'm going to put you on my back. When I do, hang on tight because we're going to be moving at top speed."

"The bloodsucker could be in those shadows!"

"He's not that close yet. But he's going to be able to smell me if he hasn't already. There's no time to waste."

"Some protection," she muttered as she followed him into the shadows. "Talk about *me* being a beacon. Why do I not feel safe walking in a haze of vampire scent?"

He surprised her with a quiet laugh, then before she realized what was happening, he'd lifted her and slung her on his back, her duffel to one side.

"Hang on," he said.

It was all the warning she got before the wind battered her face and the world began to pass in a blur. She had to press her face to his back and close her eyes against the bite of the cold wind.

Almost instantly she wished she could lift her head and face that wind and the world that seemed to be passing like an insane carousel.

Because now her awareness settled on him, on the powerful bunching of muscles she could feel through his jacket and hers, on the way her legs wrapped around his hips and how damn good it felt to have him between them.

She sensed he had climbed but he didn't pause long enough for her to look around and be certain. Not that she would have seen much.

Her traitorous body now noticed one thing and one thing only: the heaviness between her legs, how open they felt and how hard she was beginning to throb. Nearly every movement he made applied a delicious pressure that deepened the ache.

Oh, how she hoped the wind was blowing away the revealing musk and pheromones.

In less time than she could believe, they arrived at Jude's. He eased her from his back and turned to her.

He'd smelled her arousal. She could see it in the way he smiled at her. He startled her by reaching out to touch a stray lock of her hair. His golden gaze captured her, and for the first time she realized that it seemed to make promises, promises of delights beyond imagining.

She felt both a huge relief and massive disappointment when he looked away to press the buzzer. So that was how they did it, she thought almost dizzily. A simple look that seemed to promise a taste of Eden.

Clearly she wasn't immune, so she had to keep reminding herself that it was an empty promise.

Except that didn't work too well. Following him down the hallway to Jude's office, she still felt slumberous with awakened passion, and even the brush of her jeans between her legs seemed like a teasing promise.

Her skin had become exquisitely sensitive, responding even to the lightest movement of her clothes. She hurried to the couch without taking off her jacket and folded her arms and legs, trying to contain things she was sure she didn't want to feel.

Except she did. If she'd been feeling them for anyone but a bloodsucker, it would be different. They were so delicious, and they threatened to betray her.

Jude and Chloe were in the office.

"Where's Terri?" Luc asked.

"She works tonight."

Luc swore.

"It should be all right. If she has to leave the morgue, she promised to call first. I can get over there fast enough to keep an eye on her."

"And if they don't care?" Luc waved a hand, displaying more emotion than Dani had yet seen from him. "Don't you see, *mon ami?* We have at least two chinks in our armor: Terri and Dani. Both of them smell of us now, and both of them will inevitably be noticed because of it. What is more, we have to divide our attention in order to protect them. Just how do you propose to organize against them or fight them if they cause your wife to go out repeatedly to visit their crime scenes? Eh? You will spend all your time protecting and none planning. If that is the case, I suggest we all leave town right now and come back later to deal with them."

"I've sent for help. Terri is arranging tonight to take the next week off. It won't be easy, but they'll let her do it."

"In spite of this crime wave?"

"When someone in her position says she can't handle it anymore, they let them take time. It's better than having them break."

"Ah, but that leaves the little wolf here. I doubt she will find it so easy to leave her job and classes."

Dani spoke. "I said I wanted to help with this fight. I meant it." Desire had trickled into the background and with the return of her strength, she stood. "If it's necessary, I'll quit my job and drop my classes tomorrow. Luc is right, you can't have divided attention."

Had she just said that Luc was right? But he was. This was no exercise in fantasy, and she knew the threat better than anyone, having been nearly killed by four vampires who had clearly enjoyed her every scream and attempt to fight them off. However she had gotten into the middle of this war, she was squarely in it now. Stubborn, yes. But also determined. Luc's description of these rogues keeping enough humans as slaves had stiffened her backbone completely. She had only to think of her fellow students and her coworkers to know she couldn't stand back from this.

Jude nodded. "I'm not sure what you can do, but we need to clear out of here for a little while. It's no secret where I can be found, and I doubt it's a secret that Terri is my wife. Regardless, we need to wait for some others to arrive. Creed has a place north of here in the woods and he's working on it tonight to make it ready for us."

Luc stirred. "Creed is back?"

"He's most definitely back, and he's worried about Yvonne, too. So yes, we have a place to go to ground until we can organize."

Dani spoke. "What if they follow us?"

"I would much rather meet them in the woods than in town. No humans will get in the way."

Luc nodded but folded his arms and looked dubious. "And you, *mon ami?* Will you be able to live with yourself leaving this city unprotected for a few days?"

"I will have to. I can't do anything by myself. We know there are at least three. There will probably be more soon if there aren't already."

"Babies," Luc said harshly. "If they create newborns, we will have to act immediately."

Jude nodded. "I know. But at least we can leave the women in a safe place."

Dani spoke, filled with trepidation. "I can call my pack."

"No." Both vampires answered her simultaneously.

"We don't want them in the middle," Luc said. "What is more, they might not distinguish between us. Why should they? And how will you feel if they get hurt? This is not their fight."

"They're strong. Strong enough to take down a vampire."

"I know," he replied. "But a newborn is not just a vampire."

She didn't argue. How could she? She had no idea why they seemed so concerned about newborns, other than that they were simply amped-up vampires. But they *were* right about one thing: this wasn't her pack's fight—they could get hurt, and she didn't want that. What's more, unless she told them what had happened to her, they would want no part of this mess.

She pulled off her jacket, becoming uncomfortably warm now, and wondered just what she should do. Being stashed out of the way while Luc, Jude and their friends tried to deal with this didn't suit her at all. Yet she could understand how she would be a distraction if they had to worry about her.

Crap!

The earthquake had happened. Not only was she worried about the gruesome death and terror that might be inflicted on humans, but she was worried about a couple of vampires. One in particular.

Who would have imagined it?

Chapter 5

Jude picked Terri up from the morgue around three in the morning. She'd gotten her time off, and she announced as she came into the office, "It wasn't a busy night. Only two bodies."

Jude and Luc exchanged looks. "It could be," Luc said after a moment, "that the snow is keeping people indoors, making it more difficult to get at them. Or more difficult to find the bodies."

Jude nodded. "Or they've decided to change some of their victims."

"That we can't know until tomorrow night at the earliest."

"Let's pack and go," Jude said abruptly. "We still have enough time to reach Creed's cabin. We can await word on the gathering there and make plans just as well."

"What gathering?" Dani asked.

"I've been contacting old acquaintances. Some may come help."

Another gathering of vampires. Dani almost shuddered.

They drove through deepening snow, meeting almost no other traffic except plows that were trying to keep the main roads clear for morning. Their headlights bounced off swirling snow, but Jude, at the wheel, seemed to be able to see beyond it.

Maybe he could, Dani thought. She closed her own eyes so that she couldn't tell how fast they were moving when she could barely see ten feet in front of the car.

Luc sat up front beside Jude, his tense posture and the way he kept looking around telling her that while Jude drove, Luc was on sentry duty.

Beside her sat Terri, who drifted to sleep. In the rear sat Chloe, who was unusually silent.

But of course. Jude felt the danger was great enough to get the women out of town. Except for the three humans, he and Luc probably would have stayed.

Once again she was a burden to be protected. Dani's mouth soured at the thought, but realistically she had to admit there wasn't much she could do to help. She had spoken brave words, but it remained utterly beyond her to imagine how she could be anything but a hindrance.

About an hour north of the city, they turned off-road. Or maybe they were still on some road, but to Dani it looked as if they were wending their way among trees.

"How can you see where to go?" she asked finally.

"The road is there," Luc answered. "It retains a bit of heat from the sun yesterday, more than the woods beneath the trees."

"And you can see that through the snow?"

"Easily."

"My God," she muttered, once again facing the huge differences between vampires and mere humans like herself. She was surprised to feel Terri reach out and pat her forearm.

"Vampires," Terri said, "are actually quite gifted. But what's working for us now can work against us with those rogues."

"Yes," said Luc. "The passage of our car has left a heat trail for miles. I hope our departure went unobserved."

Dani couldn't even think of a reply for that. About the only equivalence she could make was her pack's ability to follow a scent even after it was weeks old, or even to follow one hundreds of feet above them in the air. She wasn't that capable herself, but she had some small experience.

These vampires magnified everything, she thought:

strength, speed, vision, smell. She most certainly didn't want her pack in the middle of this, although she felt more homesick at that moment than she had since the first days after her arrival in the city.

The cabin looked like an ordinary log cabin, albeit a large one, in a wide clearing. Only when they entered did Dani see that it was far from ordinary.

She felt as if she had stepped into some kind of bunker. The walls appeared to be solid steel; every one of the few windows was covered by heavy metal shutters. And even though there was a stone chimney outside, there was no fireplace. The door that closed behind them might have been part of a bank vault.

It was warm and furnished, however, chairs and love seats in bright colors making up as best they could for the utter lack of rustic charm.

"What is this?" she asked.

"A bunker," Luc replied.

"I can see that. But why?"

"Now that Creed has Yvonne to worry about," Jude answered, "he decided he needed a safe place to put her. The changes he made for us were mostly for you mortals' comfort."

"But why?"

Luc was suddenly in front of her, entirely too close. "When a vampire loves a human," he said, holding her with his suddenly dark gaze, "he has a weakness that can be used against him. Someone he cannot protect during the day. Ordinary precautions are not enough then."

She felt overwhelmed again by his proximity. Something in her longed to reach out and touch him, to feel him, to find out if vampire skin was warm or cold, or hard or soft. To find out if he could gentle his strength so that it wouldn't hurt her. To discover whether she fit against him.

He must have sensed it, because his gaze grew even darker. For an instant he leaned toward her. Then, quickly, he turned away.

Dani instinctively reached for her wolf's head necklace to remind herself of the gulf between them, to feel its etchings as a way to remember who and what she was. As if she really knew.

"I've had it," Chloe announced. "Where's Creed and do I get a bedroom?"

"Creed's coming back up tomorrow night. Yvonne has a meeting she couldn't miss today, and he's not on the rogues' radar yet, anyway."

"We think." Chloe sniffed. Dani thought she looked exhausted. "Bed?"

"Four bedrooms," Jude said. "Help yourself." He turned to Luc. "You two, as well. Find a comfortable place for Dani."

Luc nodded and touched her elbow, guiding her toward the back of the house. Electricity zinged through her at his touch, even though her jacket prevented it from being at all intimate.

"We're safe here, anywhere in the house," he said quietly as he guided her to the bedroom past the one Chloe entered. "You may as well enjoy a bed. You haven't had much sleep."

It was true, and even adrenaline was failing to keep her energized now that they were indoors, safe and warm. The bedroom held a large bed, a chair, a dresser, and in one wall a door led to a small bathroom. The colors were cheerful. He dropped her duffel on the foot of the bed.

"What are you going to do?" she asked, turning to him.

"In a little while, I'll be in the sleep of death. It won't matter where I am. The floor will do."

"Really?"

"Really." He gave her a half smile. "You could kill me then, little wolf."

She gasped. "No!"

A quiet laugh escaped him. "You didn't feel that way even two days ago."

She flushed, knowing he was right. But now somehow killing a vampire didn't seem quite like exterminating vermin. Yes, her pack would definitely disown her if they ever found out.

Once again Luc stood in front of her, so fast she hadn't seen him move, so close they nearly touched. Her heart slammed into high gear, but it was not from fear. If she closed her eyes, she was sure she would sway toward him, and then all her questions would be answered.

"You are so beautiful," he whispered. "You call to me, Dani Makar. As nothing has called to me in a very long time." His fingers touched her cheek, brushing the hot skin. They felt cool, but not cold.

"When you blush, you arouse me. I want to take you. Make love to you. I want to show you delights you can barely imagine. And you are curious, aren't you, little wolf? You feel the same things in a human way, but you have no idea just how I could make those feelings blossom into something you have never imagined."

She drew a shaky breath, at once excited by his words and frightened she might give in.

His fingers trailed from her cheek to her breast, brushing lightly over her nipple, which was already engorged. She sucked air, and instead of pushing him away, she tilted her head back in surrender. The desire he awoke overpowered her, drove out every bit of common sense and need to protect herself. Her entire universe centered around his gently brushing fingers, and around the hot, wet, heavy desire throbbing between her legs.

No one had ever made her feel these things. No one. As a normal, not even the potential mates among her pack and neighboring packs had ever showed the least interest in her.

But this vampire, this *bloodsucker,* was awakening her to a world she had scarcely imagined. And she wanted to taste it. For just once in her life she wanted to know what it meant to be desirable.

"I want you," he murmured. "More than you can imagine. But there is no time right now. I couldn't take you all the way before sleep claims me."

Disappointment started to crash through her. Her first response was anger, the certainty that he was lying to her, but when she met his gaze again, looked into those black depths, she knew he was being honest. His gaze had grown heavy-lidded but even more intense, almost as if he were willing her to feel what he was feeling.

She didn't know what to do or say. She had no experience with this. None. "Luc..." For the first time since meeting him, she was absolutely certain of one thing: she didn't want him to leave her alone.

He must have read the wish in her scents, in her face, somewhere. For she was in his arms almost before she knew it. He carried her to the bed, stripped off her open jacket and boots, and slipped her beneath the covers.

Then, moving slowly, almost as if he feared rejection, he stretched out beside her on top of the covers.

"Touch me," he murmured. "Learn whatever you like. I wish I had more time, but I can't resist the sleep of death for long. For this little time, I am yours, *ma belle.* Totally."

The invitation seduced her completely. Heat blossomed in her like a nuclear explosion and then her womanhood melted.

Her hand shook a little as she pulled it from beneath the covers and rolled toward him. He remained as still as if he were carved from stone, his eyes all that seemed alive. Intensely alive.

Tentatively, she touched his cheek and felt smooth skin. It was not cold skin, though it felt slightly cool. He turned his head, pressing a kiss onto her palm, then faced her again, waiting for what she would do next.

She wasn't certain. She didn't know how. But touching him was enough for now. She traced the strong bones of his face and trailed her fingers down to the throat of his shirt where she felt his pulse. Slower than hers, but strong.

He had a heartbeat. He was not dead, as her pack claimed. The dead didn't have heartbeats. Their skin wasn't this warm. Her mind whirled with the discovery.

And with it came a sense of power. The most dangerous beast of her childhood now lay beside her like a lamb, submitting to her. She knew his strength, she knew he could be dangerous, she knew he wasn't mortal, but none of that seemed important. Right now he was hers.

And if he felt anything like what he had made her feel, he was exercising immense self-control, because she knew how badly she wanted him right now. She might have torn at his clothes, feeling like this, except she had never done this before.

Fear warred with need, and fear won, barely. She didn't want to make a fool of herself by showing her inexperience, by doing something wrong.

Biting her lip, she hesitantly worked the buttons on his shirt, then pressed her palm to his bare chest.

"Ah..." he sighed. "I will tell you a small secret, *ma belle.*"

She made a questioning sound.

"The only warmth I can feel anymore is the warmth of a human touch. And it feels so very good. Keep your hand on me until I sleep. Please."

He slipped an arm beneath her, holding her close, and she didn't mind it at all. Indeed, she liked it. She rubbed her palm over his chest, listening to his satisfied sighs.

Then suddenly he stiffened, drew a sharp breath and went still.

When she looked into his face, she knew he had gone to sleep. The sleep of death, he called it.

She hesitated, then leaned forward to press an ear to his chest. She listened for a few minutes but heard nothing, no heartbeat, no breath.

She drew back a little, some atavistic response telling her to get away. But somehow she had moved past that.

She could kill him now, he had said.

Such trust left her feeling almost weak, yet incredibly powerful.

Instead, she curled a little closer until her head rested on his arm, feeling safer than she had since the attack. She'd had almost no sleep in two nights now, and some bills just had to be paid.

With her body tucked against her pack's mortal enemy, she fell into deep sleep.

Dani awoke before Luc. Her hand was still tucked within his shirt, but she felt a difference now. He was cooler, though not any colder than the room. Not by the merest twitch or breath did he show any life.

Part of her wanted to jerk back, but mostly she found questions tumbling through her mind, questions about his past, about being a vampire. Questions that her pack had ignored by treating them as the ultimate boogeymen.

So much of what she had believed had been turned upside down during the past two nights. Her pack would never believe that Luc had killed another of his kind to protect her. Never.

But she had to face facts, and that was a fact.

If her family even guessed where she was now, or that she had committed herself to taking part in a battle between vampires, they would be outraged. They might disown her. They would certainly drag her home to remind her of where her loyalties should lie.

But was she really being disloyal to her own kind by accepting that not all vampires were cold, heartless killers?

No. She had learned something, and now she simply couldn't go back to her old mindset, which had turned out to be a black-and-white view of something far more complicated.

She sighed quietly and thought about home, about how she missed it, and then with piercing certainty realized she could not return except to visit.

That was no longer her life, and the new one she was building here included a whole different view of some things.

There was no going back, not now.

All of a sudden she felt Luc's chest expand beneath her hand. Simultaneously, she heard him draw a deep, sharp breath. She looked up and saw his dark eyes snap open.

The instant he saw her, he smiled.

Helplessly, she smiled back.

"You did not flee," he murmured, as if he was surprised.

"No."

His smile deepened. He raised a hand to cover hers where it lay on his chest. "I see questions in your gaze. Ask."

She hesitated, afraid of prying, yet lying together so intimately like this seemed to invite frankness. Finally she blurted, "Are you really dead when you sleep?"

"No. That's why we're called the undead. I can wake from sleep if I must, although it's not easy. But if you were to scream my name, I would be there for you."

She flushed a little, touched that he put it in terms of protecting her. "How old are you?"

"Ah...well, do you count the years since my

change? I was forty at the time I made the choice to live rather than die at the hands of the guillotine. I flatter myself that I look a bit younger."

"You do," she agreed. "And before that?"

"What? Do you mean what was I like back then? You will never believe me."

"Why not?"

He laughed softly. "I was mostly interested in my estates. I was concerned with science and bettering my crops. I had little interest in the life at court. In short, I was rather dull. And perhaps a trifle heedless. In my quiet corner of France I thought the revolution would not reach me. I was, I believed, good to those who tilled my land and served my needs. In retrospect, I think I was not good enough. Privilege, to which I was born, can blind us to our own good fortune and the lack of fortune among others."

She considered that and nodded slowly. "I think I understand."

"You see your pack as privileged, don't you? And you feel underprivileged by comparison. It does not make you happy."

"But I wouldn't harm them!"

"No, but the situation is different, little wolf. They are your family and they cared for you enough that you love them. But I think you resent that you cannot be one of them."

A pain pierced her heart, because he was right. Definitely right. It made her feel more than a little ugly.

"So," he continued, "whether I was a good or

bad master may not have mattered as much as that the lower classes resented me because they could never achieve my rank and comforts. I cannot blame them."

"Really? You've forgiven that?"

"Over two hundred years is a long time to bear a grudge. It is so much easier to forgive."

"And now?" she asked. "How do you feel about the deal you made to change?"

"Mostly I have been glad of it, although I must confess I had very little idea of what I was agreeing to. I have mentioned the newborns. Well, I was one of them and the things I did were ugly. I will not share them. But at some point I finally realized I could not continue that way. Perhaps my conscience reasserted itself. My memories of that time are a bit confused, because learning to restrain my impulses preoccupied all my attention and will. But I learned."

He squeezed her hand. "I feel your warmth. It is a delight I never would have known as I was before. I have gained things and learned things that a mere mortal life never would have taught me. But everything is magnified. Everything. I cannot even begin to tell you how much and in what ways."

She watched his nostrils flare as if he were inhaling her, something she could totally identify with. His scent to her had become almost intoxicating. She reciprocated, drawing him into her lungs.

"Your eyes," she murmured finally, trying to retain some self-control in the face of wild sexual urges that were beginning to dominate her. "Why do they change color?"

"Ah." He shook his head a little, smiling. "My eyes grow dark when I am hungry or feeling strong emotion. When I'm content and well fed, they're golden."

"So I should pay attention?"

"You, *ma chère,* need never worry." With that he swooped in and covered her mouth with his, kissing her with an intensity her wildest imaginings had never approached. It wasn't painful, it was consuming, as if he wished to drink in her very soul. When his tongue darted between her lips and teeth, it was cool and wickedly knowledgeable, causing an unexpected cascade of yearning through her.

She would never be able to resist him. Never. That should have frightened her, but she was incapable of feeling fear amidst the heat that swamped her. When his fingers added their touch, caressing her throat and then her breast, she was lost in a haze of need more intense than anything she had ever felt.

She heard herself moan faintly, felt her body strain toward him, utterly his, wishing she could melt into him and never emerge, wishing she could stay forever in this place he had just taken her.

But as suddenly as he had lifted her to the pinnacle, he pulled back and she crashed to cold reality.

He stood now beside the bed, seeming light-years away. "I am sorry," he said quietly. "This it too dangerous."

"Dangerous?" Languid and disappointed all at once, she couldn't gather her thoughts.

"Dangerous," he repeated. "I don't want to take what you are not sure you wish to give. Nor do I ever want to claim another."

The only thing that told her he had left the room was the closing of the door. She hadn't even been able to see him move.

For a long time she couldn't seem to gather her wits or her strength. Eventually anger came to her rescue. How could he treat her like this and cast her aside? And what the hell had she been doing in the arms of a *bloodsucker?*

Anger gave her all the propulsion she needed. She jumped from the bed, washed and changed into fresh clothes. And all the while she vowed that she would find a way to put Luc St. Just in his place.

Out in the front room, she found everyone gathered. Chloe and Terri were eating something, and they pointed her to the kitchen to help herself. Coffee and some freshly baked cinnamon buns awaited her, and she realized she was absolutely famished. She hadn't finished her dinner last night and had eaten nothing since.

As she turned around to rejoin the group, however, she saw both Jude and Luc at a laptop computer. Luc stood looking over Jude's shoulder, and both of them were as still and stiff as rock.

"What is it?" she asked.

Luc turned his head. "We're alone with this."

"What?"

"The others have decided to wait before involving themselves. Creed will be here tomorrow night, but no one else is coming."

"Some friends," she remarked, her stomach sinking. All of a sudden her legs felt a little wobbly, and she made her way to the small table with difficulty.

"We have few friends," Luc said flatly. "You live in groups, but we are more solitary. Our inclinations and nature require us not to congregate."

"Why?"

"Because if too many of us live too close, we can't escape notice."

Chloe turned her coffee mug around aimlessly. "They don't get along all that well, anyway. Territorial or something. The kind of friendship that's best at a distance."

Territorialism was something Dani understood perfectly. "But surely this is different?"

Luc answered her. "Not yet. Not enough. They want to wait and see. Three of us can occupy the same city. We'd have to make a very strong cause to gather many more."

Jude spoke. "They think the three of us are enough, since there are only three rogues."

"That we know of." Luc's gaze was black as night. "There were almost no murders last night. We're trying to find out if there are reports of missing people. But right now we have nothing at all to justify the intervention of others. If there are three rogues, the three of us *should* be enough. If there are more…we shall have to prove it first."

"Yes, prove it in blood," Terri said. "How nice."

Jude answered her. "You don't have to tell me, my love."

"I know. Sorry."

Luc crossed the room and perched on the edge of a couch. "So we must plan accordingly. We must ensure the safety of the women. Then we'll have to wait another night to see if the murders multiply because of newborns."

"Why isn't Creed coming tonight?" Chloe asked.

Jude answered. "He's seeking information. As far as we know, the rogues have no quarrel with him."

Dani finally managed to sip coffee and eat her roll. Strength was important, and she was feeling entirely too weak for it to be good. But the infusion of calories began to make her feel better, and to clear the cloudiness of her brain brought on by a mixture of disappointment, desire and worry, not to mention such a long sleep.

As the mental gears began to function smoothly again, she had an idea. She struggled with it, knowing how dangerous it could be. And she certainly didn't know how she could act on it.

But it was beginning to seem necessary.

Chapter 6

The moon was bright, still nearly full. Jude and Luc decided they could all use some time outside while they waited to see what kind of news Terri could dig out of the medical examiner's office.

Luc slipped outside alone first, then returned to say there wasn't a whiff of vampire anywhere. "I think it's safe, but not everyone should go out at the same time."

"Dani first," Chloe said. "I've never been keen on tromping through deep snow. Too bad we don't have skis."

Dani went to get her jacket and gloves, and stepped outside with Luc, who was once again wearing the leathers she had first seen him in. No hat, no gloves. "Aren't you cold?"

"I can't feel temperature anymore. Hot or cold, it's all the same."

"But you said..." She trailed off, reluctant to recall the intimacy he'd cut so short so suddenly.

"I can feel your warmth. Human warmth. It's the only kind that reaches me any longer, and it's delightful."

"Wow." She waded through untrammeled snow beside him and looked up at the just-past-full moon. Right now it hung only a little above the trees, a huge silvery disk.

"What would you be doing if you were home tonight, little wolf?"

She kept her gaze on the moon as sorrow encompassed her. "Sitting beside the fire. Or maybe on the porch watching the youngsters romp."

"Why do you sound sad? You miss them?"

"Of course I miss them. What I don't miss is... Well, right now the adult pack is out running. Nights like this call to them. They'll cover fifty or sixty miles before the moon sets, howling to each other in beautiful harmony."

"And you couldn't go with them."

"No." She shook her head, trying to push away the sadness. "I never changed. Never. Most change by the time they are twelve or thirteen. I kept waiting for it to happen, but it never did. So all I could do was watch the ones who had recently changed. They weren't yet ready to travel such long distances with the pack. I was left to keep an eye on them because they are more adventurous than wise at that age."

"And the rest of the time? Did they leave you out of everything?"

"Of course not!" Angry, she stopped and glared at him. "They included me as much as they could. In fact, I think some of the members of my pack even stopped shifting as often so they could keep me company. Do you know how that made me feel?"

"It should have made you feel loved and accepted."

She almost gasped, that stung so hard. "Who are you to talk about love and acceptance?"

"I loved once," he said simply. "For a long, long time. And then she died and I went insane. I know about love."

She felt about two inches tall then. Turning, she resumed her tromp through the snow, feeling like a bitch, feeling sorrowful because it was a moonlit night, and moonlit nights had become the gauge for how she measured her inadequacy. Snow crunched beneath her boots, her tread was heavy, and all she could hear in her mind were the calls of her parents, siblings and cousins as they joyously bounded into the woods under the brilliant silver light.

An arm closed around her shoulders. "It's all right," he said.

She jerked away, blinking back tears she couldn't quite explain. "It's not okay. Nothing's okay. I'm caught up in a war I don't understand, I was nearly killed just two nights ago, I'm living with vampires, and you keep…you keep… Damn it, St. Just, don't touch me anymore if you don't mean it!"

"If I don't mean it?" He sounded astonished.

Then, much to her amazement, he seized her and the next thing she knew he was lying in the snow with her above him. Their hips met through leather and denim with excruciating intimacy. His hand held the back of her head so that their faces were separated by only inches.

"Let me tell you something, little wolf. I haven't touched a woman since my Natasha died. Not in that way. I swore I would die before I ever let another woman take the liberties she took with me, or before I ever took them with another."

"Luc…" Some part of her heart shrieked that she had to stop him now, before she learned things she didn't want to know. Things that could change her in ways she didn't want to be changed.

"Yet you draw me," he said roughly. "I break my own vow every time you are near me. But you don't understand the kind of fire we're playing with. We might escape unscathed, but I'm not sure I could stand it if we didn't."

"Then stop it," she whispered.

"I can't."

He pulled her head down and thrust his tongue into her mouth. Then, without any preamble or warning, he plunged his hand between her legs, making space for it and rubbing her most sensitive parts through denim.

There was no preventing the tide of need he unleashed in her. His knowing hand, his knowing tongue, held her in thrall. Her body ached helplessly, and she groaned into his mouth as her hips helplessly answered the rhythm of his hand.

Electrified, she could only give in.

The ache grew, everything else vanished. She was riding him to the stars like Pegasus, to a paradise she had never visited. All she knew for certain was that she needed more, and more....

Dimly she felt the zipper of her jacket lower, felt the neck of her sweater tugged aside. He dragged his mouth from hers and she tipped her head back, sucking in the frigid night air as the pressure built closer to a crescendo.

Vaguely she felt him lick the skin just below her collarbone. Another shiver of absolute delight filled her and then something beyond imagining happened.

She felt him as if he were her. She could feel his hunger, every bit as huge as her own. She felt his heart as if it were her own, and felt them fall into exactly the same rhythm.

His desire became hers and fueled her pounding need until she thought she would shatter before it was fulfilled.

His hips thrust up against hers, crushing his hand

between them, and at that moment she exploded like a supernova, every bit of her being flying out among the stars.

Slowly she came back to herself. She was still lying on him, but now his arms were wrapped around her. She could feel cold snow melting into the knees of her jeans, but she didn't care. Her head rested on his shoulder, and she wanted to keep it there forever.

"Wow," she whispered.

"Yes," he agreed, but there was something in his tone that didn't sound quite as happy as she felt.

"What happened?" she asked weakly, not at all sure she wanted to know.

"I did something wrong."

"How could anything that good possibly be wrong?"

"I drank from you," he said baldly. "Without your permission."

"What?" Adrenaline flooded her, driving away all the wonderful magic he had just given her. She sat up, hardly caring that she sat on him, and looked down at him. His eyes were as golden as any wolf's. "You drank from me?"

"Yes. Only a little, but yes."

Fear clutched her. "Will I change?"

"You didn't change when you were attacked. Drinking from you is nothing but drinking from you. It harms you in no way."

She felt she ought to get furious. He had taken her blood without asking. That was wrong, definitely. Somehow. But she couldn't quite figure out how, considering what they had just done. Just that in some deep way, she felt it was wrong. But…

"Is that…is that why I felt as if you were part of me?"

"Yes. I felt you in the same way. It multiplies the pleasure."

"Whoa." She lifted her hand to her head, feeling as if the world were turning upside down again. She should be spewing rage, but she wasn't. How could she be when she had enjoyed every single moment? But she ought to be.

Shouldn't she?

Struggling with herself, she tried to get to her feet. At once Luc sat up and helped her. Standing facing him in the snow with the moon rising overhead, feelings ping-ponged around inside her like a mad game of table tennis.

"You shouldn't have done that," she said sharply. Except that she was sure it had enhanced the incredible experience. Never before had she heard of two hearts beating as one except in sappy songs.

"No," he agreed.

"Promise you won't do it again without asking."

"I promise."

But she saw amusement in the curvature of his mouth and snapped, "What's so funny?"

"I won't have to ask you," he said. "Now that you know, you'll ask me."

That was just too much. "Over my dead body," she snapped, then turned to storm back to the house.

Every single step of the way she was aware of him right behind her.

And aware that he was right. She already wanted him again.

Consternation grew. There was only one murder that night.

"They're building an army," Luc said. "An army of newborns."

Terri spoke. "You can't be sure of that, Luc. Given the weather, a lot of people are staying at home. It may be that some of the killings haven't been discovered yet."

"Perhaps. But if I were them, I'd build an army of newborns if I truly wanted to unleash terror."

"How long will it take?" Dani asked.

"There's some blessing," Jude answered. "It can take one or two nights for a newborn to fully change. But more important, no vampire can change more than one human a night."

"Why?"

Luc looked at her. "Because we must give our own blood to those we would change. No more than one a night. Sometimes no more than one every two or three nights."

"So it would take time?"

"I think," he said drily, "that we can still breed faster than rabbits."

"Understatement," Chloe said sarcastically. "It would be a geometric progression, wouldn't it? Each new vampire makes another one each night?"

Jude shook his head. "No, because newborns drink their victims dry and almost never think to change them. They're too voracious."

"Small mercies," Chloe muttered.

"Even supposing the rogues can change only one a night," Luc said, "it still results in a large crop of maddened vampires rather quickly. And we don't know how many rogues we're dealing with. It could be more than three." He looked at Jude. "There must be more murders. They need to replenish after each change."

Jude frowned. "True."

"Unless they've found their way into a blood bank," Terri said, "we can expect increasing reports of victims found at home."

Silence filled the room. Apparently no one wanted to contemplate what they might learn over the coming nights.

"I need to call my family," Dani announced, seizing the moment.

"Why?" Jude asked.

"Because they've got to be hearing about this. I need to reassure them, and it's been too long since I called. But my cell doesn't work here."

"There's a landline," Jude said, pointing. "Go ahead."

"Not before dawn. On a night like this, they're out running."

"Help yourself whenever."

So that was taken care of, she thought. After everyone went to sleep at dawn, she could make her call. She just hoped she wasn't making the biggest mistake of her life.

But one thing she knew for sure: if other vampires wouldn't come, and this thing kept snowballing, a lot of people were going to die. Regardless of the enmity between her kind and vampires, she hoped her pack wouldn't want to stand by while humans were being slaughtered and changed. Her strongest argument was that a world taken over by rogue vampires would be the worst possible outcome, even for lycanthropes.

She just hoped she could make them understand.

Luc gave her a rueful look but didn't say a word when he headed off to bed and she made no move to follow. Terri and Jude went at the same time. Chloe spent a few minutes making sure Dani could keep track of the news on the laptop, then wended her own way to her bedroom.

Dani waited, on the edge of her seat, until she was sure not only the vampires had fallen asleep. Then she picked up the phone and called her mother.

"Hi, Mom."

Lucinda Makar sounded drowsy, as was to be expected after a full night of running with the pack, but delighted to hear her daughter's voice. "I've been thinking about you so much, Dani. What kind of city did you move to?"

"A really nice one until a few days ago."

"There must be some really horrible gang running around down there. Do they have any idea when they'll catch them?"

Dani bit her lip and squeezed her eyes closed. "That's what I called about. Mom, I need your help. I need the pack's help. And you're not going to like it."

"Have you been hurt?"

"I'm fine." True, but not the whole truth. "Mom, please, you've got to listen and you've got to listen carefully before you start getting mad or yelling for Dad to talk sense to me. Please."

A silence greeted her, but finally Lucinda sighed. "I'm sure I'm not going to like this, but yes, I'll listen first."

"All the way through?"

"All the way through."

With her heart in her throat, Dani explained, beginning with the fact that a vampire had saved her life and had killed the bloodsucker who had come to kill her. She could hear her mother almost spluttering with the effort of keeping quiet.

"Just listen," she begged again. "Please, just listen."

"You should have come straight home."

"I can't. And that's why you have to listen."

She had known it wouldn't be easy. Given her family's beliefs about vampires, she had to keep coming back to the fact that a vampire had saved her and that two of them were protecting her. Then she had to explain the rogues and the difference between them and Jude and Luc, and apparently many others.

Her words seemed to be falling into an abyss of silence.

She pressed on anyway, making her point as forcefully as she could: either these rogues were stopped or tens of thousands of humans would eventually die, and the world would become a much more dangerous place for the packs.

"I need your help," she finished. "*We* need your help."

Lucinda didn't answer immediately. Then, "Your father is going to be furious. I don't know if I'll be able to restrain him or the pack."

"You can. I know you can." In the pack the alpha female ruled, and her mother was the alpha.

"I don't know," Lucinda said. "What I can tell you is we'll be there tonight to judge the situation for ourselves."

"There's nothing to judge! I've done that already."

"You think you have, but persuading the others will take more than that. Where exactly are you?"

"At a cabin in the country north of the city. I don't

know exactly." Then she had a thought. "I'm sitting at a computer. Maybe I can find out."

"Find out by the time we arrive later. I mean that, Dani. And don't be surprised if your father calls you back. Is this a landline?"

"Yes."

"Well, I have the number. I'm sure we can find out where it's located. Just don't do another thing until we get there."

Dani disconnected. Then she put her head in her hand and prayed she hadn't just made things worse.

Chloe's voice startled her. "I can't believe you just did that!"

She turned around to see Chloe looking like an angry goddess in some kind of black drape.

"Are you nuts? As if Jude and Luc don't already have their hands full enough, you called in your wolf pack?"

"They'll help," Dani said, because she had to believe it.

"Help how? They loathe vampires. What in the world do you think is going to change their minds?"

"Luc saved me."

"Right, and that's going to stop them from ripping his head off how? Especially when they can probably smell him all over you."

Dani flushed. Was it that obvious, so obvious a human could pick up on it? "They'll listen to me."

"Right. And I suppose you were going to spring

this on everyone when your pack showed up howling at the door for blood?"

"Chloe..."

"This is stupid. *Stupid!* You just made the mess bigger than it already was." Chloe whirled and stomped down the hall, calling over her shoulder, "And if you think I'm going to let them sleep all day and wake up to this mess without warning, you're wrong."

Moments later, she heard Chloe hammering on doors and shouting at the top of her lungs, "Jude! Luc! Wake up. It's urgent."

Dani had the worst urge to flee as she realized she was about to face two irate vampires. They had told her not to do this, with good reason. But she couldn't stand the thought of them, and this Creed she had never met, facing all these rogues and possibly newborns alone.

The sun was up, although none of its light was permitted to invade the cabin, and despite all stories to the contrary, two vampires emerged into the living room looking fully alert and awake. Terry trailed after them, but she looked sleepy.

"What's going on, Chloe?" Jude asked.

"This...this *semiwolf* just called her pack down here. She thinks they'll help."

Dani winced, but forced herself to keep silent.

Luc came to her and knelt before her, taking her hands with surprising gentleness. "Why, Dani? We warned you not to."

"You need help. The other vampires won't come, and it's getting worse and worse. My pack…my pack ought to help. They're the only help we can get."

"*If* they help," Jude said harshly.

Luc was frowning at her, clearly troubled. "Why would you do such a thing without telling us?"

"Because you kept saying no. And you kept talking about all the newborns and people dying, and what good are my pack if they won't protect people?"

"They'll protect *people,*" he said tautly. "But they won't protect *us*. Pah!" He dropped her hands and rose, striding across the room, his back to her.

"I'll talk to them," Dani pleaded. "I'll go out and talk to them when they arrive. Just trust me."

"When they arrive," Luc said sternly, "they'll be maddened by the scent of vampire that clings to you. You'll be lucky if they don't attack *you.*"

"You don't know them! They're not like that."

"No?" He faced her, and she didn't know which upset her more, the look of betrayal on his face or the bleakness of his black eyes. "When they arrive, wake us before you do anything else. Wash yourself well. Then go out to meet them."

"And then?"

"And then when you discover that all they want to do is kill us, leave with them. Leave with them, go back north with them and stay away."

With that he vanished down the hall. She heard the door close emphatically behind him.

She felt a tear roll down her cheek but didn't bother to dash it away. She'd tried to do something good, but had alienated Luc. And maybe the rest of them, as well.

She looked from one face to another and read only dismay. Maybe even distrust. Another huge tear followed the first.

"I'm sure," said Jude finally, "that you meant well. But we may now have far more trouble than we had to begin with. Do as Luc said. Wash and meet them alone. If they can't agree to at least a truce, then leave with them. I mean it."

Then Dani was alone again. She began to weep, wondering how it was that she had fallen into an abyss between two worlds.

Inside, she had never felt more empty or alone.

Chapter 7

Twilight came at last. She had bathed as Luc had told her and changed her clothes. Nothing, however, could rub the smell of vampire from her jacket.

No one emerged from the bedrooms, even though she expected them, judging the light conditions by the time.

And then she heard it. Even through the walls of this bunker, she could hear the howls of her pack. Each wolf's song was familiar to her, tied to a name. Tied to someone she loved. That they had chosen to come in this form rather than their human form told her much.

This could be a fight she lost.

She went to stand on the porch to await them, her

heart hammering, her knees weak. Behind her she heard someone lock the door.

Closing her out of their lives. Protecting themselves against her and what she had done.

She wanted to sag, but forced herself to stiffen, to stand straight, to appear sure.

The first wolf burst into the clearing from among the trees. Her father, readily recognizable by his black coat and massive size. Lycanthropes became wolves of exactly the same size as the humans they were the rest of the time. Her father was a powerful man, well over six feet tall, and two hundred pounds of pure muscle.

He stopped at the clearing's edge and lifted his snout, smelling the night. Then he issued a low, long howl and others followed. Her mother, petite by comparison, yet larger than an ordinary wolf, her coat colors of silver, white and caramel. The colors of her mask looked like a perpetual smile.

Then her four brothers, nearly as big as their father, in every shade from white to black. She could hear others in the woods, but only the six emerged, the rest waiting to see if they were needed.

Her father approached her first, sniffing closely about her, so big that when he lifted his head he could look her in the eyes. Twice he snorted, as if displeased.

Then came the other five, first her mother and then her four brothers. They swirled around her, using their acute sense to read things she could only guess at because she wasn't really one of them.

Her mother nudged her until she stepped off the porch and into the snow, away from the cabin. She reached out to touch fur with all the love she felt for them, and ached when they each dodged her touches.

She knew what they smelled on her.

Then, in a motion so smooth it almost seemed like melting, her father and mother transformed into humans. It was not, however, a full transformation. Their bodies remained covered with sleek fur since they had brought no clothes.

"I smell them all over you," her father said. "Why, daughter? Why?"

"I told Mom. One of them saved my life. I've learned, Dad. Not all vampires are what we thought. Some of them are actually fighting to save humans."

"Your mother told me. I'm not sure I believe any bloodsucker could be good."

"Jerrod," her mother said quietly. "I told you what she said. If she's right, we can't just take her from here. We might need to help."

"Help bloodsuckers?" Jerrod practically thundered the words.

"Yes," said Dani, lifting her chin. "At first I thought a war between vampires would be a good thing. And then I saw what the rogues are doing, and what the vampires who protect me are doing differently. I thought of what it would mean to the packs if the rogues win and take over. Father, listen to me.

Imagine a world overrun by vampires who are fed by human slaves. What would that mean to the pack?"

"That's what they already do!"

"No," Dani said firmly. "Believe me. Think about it. If it were already that way, how is it so many humans survive? And when was the last time we were ever attacked by a vampire?"

"They stay out of our way."

"They have no quarrel with us."

Her father started to speak again, but her mother touched his arm. "Wait. Think. Dani may have a point."

She looked at Dani. "Are any of them brave enough to come out?"

"They thought you would take me away with you. They weren't happy I asked for your help. They expected a reaction like Dad's."

At that her mother smiled faintly. "I wonder why. Call one of them out."

Dani started to turn back to the house, but just then Luc stepped out through the door and closed it behind him. He stood on the porch, surveying the visible pack members, sniffing the air.

"Eau de wolf," he said sardonically. "Everywhere." Then he stepped off the porch and approached slowly. "I am Luc St. Just. I found your daughter nearly dead in the park and saved her from the vampire who came back to finish her off. I regret this does not match your beliefs about us. I must have been in an off mood that night."

Dani sucked a sharp breath, wondering if he meant to be provoking.

Her father sniffed. "Bloodsucker. Why is your smell all over my daughter?"

Lucinda looked at her. "Dani!" she said, sounding horrified.

"The cabin is small," Luc said with a nonchalant shrug. "I'm sure her odor is all over me. I took nothing from her she didn't offer. Well, perhaps a teaspoon of blood."

In an instant Jerrod became a wolf again and started to spring, but Dani stepped in front of Luc. "If you harm him, you have to harm me first."

Jerrod twisted in midflight and landed on all fours. Moments later he was an almost-man again. "What is going on here?"

"I told Mom and I'm sure she told you. We need your help. Humans need your help. These vampires need your help to prevent the ugliest of their kind from taking over. You said you'd been reading about the murders. Well, we're getting ready to fight the rogues, but they're probably busy making more vampires. Think of it, Dad. Is that really the world you want?"

He didn't answer.

"Because if that's the world you want," Dani said firmly, "then leave now and I'll stay to fight with these people."

"You call vampires people?"

"Now I do. A handful at least."

He shook his head.

But Lucinda moved forward, looking past Dani at Luc. "You saved my daughter?"

"It was my honor."

"And you killed her attacker?"

"Quite delightfully. I gutted him and broke his neck."

To Dani's amazement, her mother began to smile. "That would have pleased me."

"It certainly pleased *me.*"

Dani's brothers were swirling around all of them now, clearly uneasy, but equally uncertain. Her father growled but made no move.

Lucinda turned to her mate. "Will you take her from the only world where she might fit, Jerrod? You know how unhappy she was with us."

Dani started to protest, even though there was a certain truth to her mother's words. Lucinda silenced her with a look.

"So what are you saying?" Jerrod asked.

"I suggest we relax and look into the matter before deciding anything."

Jerrod looked at Luc. "How many bloodsuckers are here?"

"Just myself and one other, plus two other humans. And we expect one more of our kind sometime tonight. So you can identify him and leave him alone, he'll be arriving with another human female."

"His slave?"

"His wife."

Jerrod made a rumbling sound of disbelief, but then fell silent.

"A truce," Lucinda said finally. "For tonight. If we decide against you, we'll leave with our daughter and leave you untouched."

"Fair enough," said Luc. "I'll tell the others."

Lucinda returned her attention to Dani. "I'm not sure you're being wise, but you have your chance to explain. We'll be back in a few minutes. We left our clothes in the car."

Then she and Jerrod melted back into wolf form and dashed into the woods, their sons following them.

"Well," said Luc almost sarcastically. "That went far better than I hoped."

Dani dared to look at him. "Do you hate me?"

"No. But I'm not very pleased. This could have turned bloody."

She knew he was right. And it might still turn bloody, but not tonight. Her mother had given her word, and Lucinda's word was better than gold.

Twenty minutes later a car pulled up to the cabin and disgorged Lucinda and Jerrod, a handsome couple dressed in heavy wolfskin parkas and boots. Somewhere out there her brothers and cousins still lurked watchfully, but for now there was a truce.

Only Jerrod hesitated to cross the threshold of the cabin. "This place reeks of bloodsuckers."

"Hardly surprising," Luc said. "And now it reeks of wolf, as well."

Dani scowled at him. Being provocative was not the best way to deal with her pack. She noted that both he and Jude stood closest, while Chloe and Terri remained back in the kitchen area. For nearly a minute, no one moved, then Terri swept forward.

"Coffee?" she said cheerfully. "I can also make something to eat if you're hungry."

Lucinda studied her, then smiled. "Coffee would be nice. We feel the cold more in human form."

The room felt as electric as the air before a thunderstorm. While the coffee brewed, a lot of uneasy shifting took place, but at last the humans and the wolves settled at the table with mugs. The vampires hung back, adopting relaxed poses but not getting too close.

"All right," Lucinda said. "I know what Dani told me. We've read news reports of the murders and were becoming concerned for her, but nothing made us think of vampires."

"It was vampires, all right," Dani said. She looked at Jude. "Can you explain? You do it better than I can."

"And I'm at the heart of what's going on," he said. He came closer to the table. "When I arrived in the city I set about cleaning it out." Then, steadily, as if listing bullet points in a presentation, he laid out his philosophy of never harming humans and explained that the view was shared by most vampires, for their own safety if nothing else. "But in cleaning out the city, I evidently made some enemies. Now they've come back to inflict a reign of terror and probably to kill me and anyone else who resists them."

Luc also came closer. "They want to run the show. They don't want to resist their native impulses, not even a little bit."

"But can they succeed?"

"Here?" Luc asked. "Certainly. No others will come to our aid yet, and I suspect they are making newborns. Newborns, by the way, are the embodiment of the worst you think of all my kind. If not carefully controlled by their makers, they become berserk killers."

Lucinda looked down for a minute, then turned to Dani. "You believe this?"

"Completely."

"And you want our help against these rogues and newborns?"

Dani bit her lip. "Mom, these three can't do it alone. Would the packs be safe if vampires rule?"

"You know we never involve ourselves in the affairs of other kinds."

"I know." She felt her heart sinking.

Lucinda looked at the two vampires. "We prefer to live in solitude and let others go their own ways."

"I prefer that also," Luc said. "This time, however, order must be restored before chaos consumes us all."

"How would you have us help?"

"I don't know," Luc answered. "I wasn't the one who called for you. Initially I had no desire to get involved in this war. I simply came to warn Jude the rogues were coming after him. Then I saw what they did to Dani. I must admit, madam, that it made me angry. Angry enough that I decided to involve myself in what is surely not *my* problem. I could have left it to others."

It was almost a challenge, and Dani tensed as she waited to see how her mother would react. But if ever she had doubted Luc had been a marquis, she could believe it then. There was a certain arrogant surety to what he was saying. She just hoped it didn't drive her family away.

Lucinda spoke quietly. "You turned your back on a problem once. You thought it didn't involve you."

Luc's face tightened. "Yes. I did."

She nodded. "It haunts you."

"In more ways than you can imagine."

Lucinda finished her coffee and rose from the table. "I'll call my pack together. I'll tell them we're going to help you. Part of that will require that you allow the entire pack to smell you so they don't mistake you for the others."

"And then what will you do, madam?"

"Hunt vampires."

She nodded to everyone in the room and headed for the door, Jerrod beside her. "Dani. I wish a private word."

Dani followed her parents outside, feeling very

small, very young and unsure of herself. But lack of confidence was nothing new to her. She'd felt it for years and had only just started to shake it after her move to the city and living among humans. Just having her family back around her, though, was enough to remind her of all her inadequacies. She thrust her hand inside the neck of her parka to grasp her wolf's head necklace, a reminder that her mother loved her despite her decision to leave the pack.

Lucinda sent Jerrod away. "Gather the others. Send for the rest and bring them up to speed."

Jerrod hesitated only a moment, looking as if he had plenty he wanted to say to Dani, but then he returned to the car and drove back into the woods, where he would no doubt strip and transform again. The pack communicated far more readily as wolves, and far more clearly.

Her mother turned to look at her. "You looked more powerful when we arrived. You *smelled* more powerful."

Dani couldn't deny it. "I feel like a pup again."

Lucinda reached out to cup her cheek gently. "Daughter, don't do this to yourself. You're an adult, you had the courage to leave the pack and strike out to make your own life. How many of *us* would dare that?"

Not many, Dani admitted to herself. When the packs grew too large, as occasionally happened, they split. But never did one wolf go off by itself. Never.

"You're not like us, but there's nothing wrong

with that, Dani. If we ever made you feel there was, I'm sorry."

"You didn't make me feel that way."

"But being unable to change and become one of us certainly did. You are who you are, and who you are is sufficient. We love you as you are."

"I know." Her throat tightened with the truth of it. "I never felt unloved."

"I should hope not. But now I'm worried."

"Why?"

"Because of that vampire. Luc. I feel something between the two of you." Lucinda frowned. "Dani, if you go that way, I can't guarantee the packs won't shun you. I may plead for sense, but some things are deeper than logic."

Dani swallowed hard. She thought about Luc, about what had passed between them, and realized that all that had really happened was lust. Hormones and pheromones and not one other thing. It hurt to look at it clinically, but she had to be honest with herself.

"Nothing will come of it," she said finally. "Nothing. I don't think he likes me all that much, actually."

"Like?" Lucinda almost laughed. "That vampire came out here to keep an eye on you. I could smell it all over him. He thought we might attack you because you smell like them now. He was ready to take on our entire pack if anyone made a threatening gesture toward you."

"How can you tell that? I couldn't smell it."

"I could. I could also see it in the way he emerged from the cabin. His every muscle was coiled. You didn't see it because your back was turned."

"He's protective," Dani said reluctantly.

"More than that, perhaps. I don't know. I just know that if you take up his way of life, you will probably lose ours."

"Mom..."

"Not me, Dani, never me. But there are some things not even an alpha can command. Our loathing of vampires can be restrained, but only for a while. Just keep that in mind. And don't let him drink from you again."

Dani, who remembered those brief moments as a trip to the stars, said nothing, just nodded an acknowledgment.

"Protect *him* by keeping a proper distance," Lucinda warned her. "If the others think he's put you under his spell, they will tear him to pieces."

"He can't affect me that way."

"Are you absolutely sure of that?" Lucinda's smile was almost sad as she turned away.

"What are you going to do now?"

"I think we'll go to the city and check things out."

Dani's heart squeezed with fear. What had she set in motion? "If the rogues smell you..."

"We will deal with them. That's what you wanted, isn't it?" Then she ran into the woods and disappeared from sight.

"Oh, my God." The tormented whisper squeezed

out from between Dani's lips, and her knees gave way. She sank to the snow and started to cry.

Never, ever had she considered the possibility her pack might act alone.

Luc finally grew impatient and opened the front door. He saw Dani huddled in the snow, heard her nearly silent sobs, smelled her distress on the clear, cold air.

He told himself to step back, give her time to deal with whatever was going on. He was still more than a little annoyed that the wolves had been thrown into the equation after both he and Jude had told her to keep them out of it.

They were an unknown and might complicate an already complicated problem. They still hadn't even learned what they were up against in terms of how many and what kind. Absent that knowledge, absent any other vampires arriving unless the situation worsened, they still hadn't been able to put together a plan.

Now this.

Yes, he was annoyed. But the sounds issuing from Dani reached the heart that he had tried so hard to turn into stone, so he went to her.

He scooped her up out of the snow, sat cross-legged and put her on his lap, shielding her from the icy ground with his impervious body.

The crack in the shell around his heart grew even wider when she turned into him and wrapped an arm around him. God, he didn't want to feel again. But what he wanted didn't change what was. It never did.

Anger seeped out of that crack. "What did she say to you? Did she hurt you?"

"Not intentionally." Dani hiccuped. "I'm scared, Luc. They're going into town to check the situation out. What if I got them all killed?"

He could have made a brittle and sharp comment about how she should have thought of that first, but he didn't. She had acted out of the best intentions, and it just wasn't in him to criticize someone for that. He'd certainly made enough mistakes of his own.

"I'm sure they'll take care." It was a lame reassurance, but there was no other.

"Yes, but still… They can smell the vampires, Luc, but you certainly know that the vampires can smell them."

"True," he admitted.

"And it's my fault they're taking this risk."

"Not your fault," he said. "They chose to do this."

"For me."

"Not just for you. They know they could have taken you home whether you liked it or not. Tell me that's not true."

She couldn't. She hiccuped again and swiped at her cheeks.

"They decided to become involved the way I did not two centuries ago. They did it to prevent the kind of chaos that would make life impossible for them. And for humans."

"I hope so."

"Of course they did. It was your mother who instantly picked up on my regrets. She could have done that only if she saw far enough down the road to realize the regrets the pack would feel if they didn't act. She's farsighted."

"She has to be."

"I'm sure she'll take every precaution because if what you said is correct, they want to assess the situation, not start the battle tonight. And I'll tell you something else, little wolf."

"What's that?"

"In human form, they don't much smell like wolves. So the rogues shouldn't catch scent of them unless they prowl in wolf shape. And even then they don't smell all that different from true wolves. To identify the difference, you have to have been exposed to it before, and the packs, as you say, avoid that."

"Really?"

"Really."

That eased her heart a bit.

"I doubt the rogues expect any intervention from lycanthropes. If your family is careful, they shouldn't alert the—how do you say?—the bad guys."

"I hope not."

"Your mother is wise. She could tell we had very

little intelligence about the situation. And we really don't. We know they want Jude. We had to protect three females, and so we decamped to find backup and try to gather enough information to make some kind of plan."

"How can you plan something like this?"

"Very carefully." He sighed and brushed cool fingers against her cheek. "If you want, I can go to town and keep an eye on your pack. Unfortunately, I'm fairly certain I left *my* scent on that rogue I killed. I may draw unwanted attention. But still, I could be a distraction if needed."

That thought terrified her as much as what her pack might face. "You can't. The rest of the pack doesn't know your smell. You could be in danger."

"I think I smell enough like you to be safe."

"No," she said again, almost desperately. She had enough to worry about without adding him to the mix. Everything she cared about out there and exposed in that city? No way. "If you go, you can't go without me. I'm all that would stand between you and my pack."

"And you can't stop me from going without you."

She lifted her face, meeting his gaze directly. "No, I can't. But you can't prevent me from following you on my own."

He sighed then, really sighed. "You are difficult."

"I know."

A smile twitched around the edges of his mouth. "I am not used to being thwarted."

"Sometimes I can see that. Get used to it."

"I'm learning."

She scrubbed at her face with her sleeve, drying the last of her tears. "They'll be okay."

"Your mother strikes me as one who will ensure they do nothing to draw attention. But I can understand why she wants to evaluate the situation. We need to know what we're up against, and trying to discern that from what Terri can learn from the medical examiner's office and police reports...that's not enough."

"They can run fast," she said as her emotions settled, the storm over. "They can sample the air and be out of there quickly. Do you know how many vampires are usually there?"

"Jude would know, but not I."

"Then maybe we can get a sense of how the numbers have grown."

"That would be helpful. Very helpful."

She nodded and sniffled down the last of her tears.

He shifted restlessly beneath her. Her proximity was driving him nearly mad with lust and hunger, and that, when added to his impatience, was making him acutely aware of a need for action.

He could have laughed at himself. He had thought the centuries had taught him patience. Maybe about some things. But not about what was going on now.

He wanted to take action against the threat. Being stymied because they were essentially blind and could find no help from other vampires was not at all to his taste.

He could, of course, just leave as he had initially intended to. But ignoring an ugly situation once had cost him much, and time had taught him the full toll of his mistakes. He wasn't inclined to repeat them.

"You must be freezing," Dani said, withdrawing her arm in order to look at him.

He felt that small withdrawal in places he thought Natasha's death had killed. "I could sit in the snow all night and not freeze. I really do not feel it."

"So you weren't exaggerating?"

"Why would I? I told you, I'm impervious to temperature. The only heat I can feel is the warmth of a human body."

"That seems odd."

"Every predator is drawn to particular prey. I assume there are reasons for them all."

"Oh."

Well, he thought, perhaps he had just passed the shock factor with her. Now she would realize that while he wasn't the creature of myth her family had taught her, he was still as far as possible from anything she could imagine. And it wouldn't hurt for her to remember he was indeed a predator. Her family was not wrong about that.

"Is that how you see yourself?"

"It's not a matter of how I see myself. I *am* a predator. The fact that I choose to limit myself to willing donors doesn't change my essential nature."

"My pack are predators, too," she said presently. "They hunt deer, elk and other game. I never hunted. I couldn't."

He wondered where she was trying to go with this, but she didn't say any more. The heavy need was growing in him, pounding relentlessly in his veins. Even as bundled up as she was, he could smell her blood, a sweet siren's call. His gaze focused on her neck, exposed just a little because she hadn't zipped her jacket all the way. It would be all too easy to give a little tug to that fabric and expose her delicious flesh. To lean forward and sip. Just a small sip. Just one.

"Luc!"

The call from the door shook him out of the intoxication that was overtaking him. In a single fast movement, he rose and set Dani on her feet.

Jude was calling to them. "We've learned some more."

He was sure the news wasn't good.

"Creed," Jude said as they gathered around the table and the computer, "has identified at least eight adults and three newborns new to the city. Terri thinks other newborns may awake tonight in their homes or in the morgue."

"Yes," Terri said. "I've told my staff to start autopsies immediately on any new bodies brought in. That it's essential to do craniotomies first."

"Pardon?" Luc said.

"To remove the brains. I told them I suspect some

infection is being passed that may show up in the brains. They're thinking rabies. I'm leaving it at that."

But even as she spoke, Luc noticed she was pulling on her outerwear.

"I've got to get back. I have to make sure we don't risk letting any newborns awake in the morgue. I can't do anything about private homes, but I can damn well make sure we change the order of procedures from here on out. We'll do our part. I just don't want to risk someone overlooking or ignoring the change. That could wind up being deadly."

"And at nightfall," Jude agreed. "I'm taking her back."

"I'm going, too," Luc said.

"Me, too," Dani announced. "My pack went into town to try to sniff out vampires."

Jude swore. "I thought we had an alliance going here, not a helter-skelter, do-as-you wish operation!"

"You don't tell an alpha what to do."

"Maybe not. But if you go into town, how in the hell are we going to get in touch with your pack and let them know where we are? How are we going to exchange information?"

"My mother has a phone," Dani said tautly.

"Well, she better be answering."

"Jude," Terri said quietly. "Please. I know you don't want me going back to town, but surely you understand that I have to. And you shouldn't take your anger out on Dani."

Jude turned to Chloe. *"You,"* he said, "stay here. I'm going to have my hands full enough trying to keep my wife safe."

"Trust me, boss," Chloe said, "I don't plan on going back. I'll be here. If the pack comes here, I'll pass along the information. But exactly where are you all going to be?"

"I'll be at the morgue with Terri at least until dawn. Luc, if Dani insists on going back, take her to Creed. At least he's not a target. Yet."

"Yet," Luc agreed. He turned to Dani. "Try to reach your mother. When you do, tell her we're meeting at Creed's. I'll give you the address." He smiled almost sardonically. "And thus ends Creed's honeymoon. I'm sure he'll be delighted to have to share his bedroom with another vampire."

"He knows you're coming," Jude said. "He could have objected if he wanted. He wants me there, too. He doesn't think my office is safe. They've been sniffing around, according to him."

"Then we shall all meet there."

Ten minutes later all of them except Chloe were in the car, heading into the unknown.

Chapter 8

The drive back to the city sped by, mostly because the snow had long since stopped and the roads were clear. There was little enough talk, but the tension in the car was palpable.

Luc had folded himself into the backseat with Dani, and Terri sat up front beside Jude. Neither vampire seemed at all happy with the turn of events.

Not that Dani was. But on the way back she could feel an almost palpable gulf between her and Luc, bigger than what she had felt just the night before. Admittedly she had complicated their lives by bringing her pack in on this. As scared as she was, she wasn't sure she had been wrong.

But Luc probably thought so, and it made her ache to think he might be mad at her. Even the comfort he had offered such a short time ago as they sat in the snow seemed to have been temporary, and to have drifted into the past somehow.

It was Jude who broke the silence. "You're going to be in serious danger, Terri. If those rogues figure out that you're thwarting them by killing the newborns before they can awake, they're going to want you with a vengeance."

"They can't get at me during daylight. By tomorrow night I should have everyone in the morgue convinced to do the brain studies first."

"I hope so. Because that's the last place I want you to be tomorrow night. By then they may figure out that something is going wrong with newborns."

Luc spoke. "The morgue might actually be a good place to meet them first. Assuming we want to draw them out. If they go there to protect the newborns or to find out what's going wrong, we can prepare."

"Good thinking," Jude said.

Dani raised a question. "So when you set out to change someone, it never fails?"

"Never," Luc answered. "No one has ever heard of a case. So they'll know someone is interrupting the process somehow, and the easiest place to look first is at the morgue."

"But there must be others who won't be found until it's too late."

"Clearly," he answered, his voice heavy. "Clearly."

She longed to reach out to him. To take his hand and feel a reassuring squeeze from his fingers, but when she looked at him, the moonlight trailing through the windows told her that he was as rigid and unyielding as a statue.

He couldn't blame her for Terri's having to go back. That was clearly her decision. So he must be angrier than he had let on about her bringing in her pack. But she didn't know how to ask. Nothing about him invited questioning, and certainly not about a topic that had become so important. Or maybe she didn't want to hear the answer.

"Try again," he said shortly.

So she tried her mother again. No answer. "I'll call her in the morning. In town they'll prefer human shape when it's light." She didn't want to think about all the other reasons her mother might not be answering. Couldn't bear to think about them. She had to believe the pack had spread out and was taking an inventory of the scents around the city.

"Leave her a message with Creed's address," Luc said. "At least let her know in case she plans to head back to the cabin."

So Dani dialed again, hoping against hope that this time her mother would answer. Instead, she was thrown into voice mail and she repeated the message and the address Luc gave her.

Then the car went utterly silent again.

Finally, deep in the downtown area, Jude swung the car into an underground lot.

"Do you want me to come to the morgue with you?" Luc asked.

"I don't think it's necessary, but I'll call you if something happens. Take care of Dani. And someone who knows what's going on has to be ready to deal with the pack when they arrive."

Dani could have done that. She just didn't want to be that far from Luc. And she was disturbed that he apparently felt he could leave her in the care of another. Then she told herself to stop being so juvenile. Neither of them had committed to anything except seeing this mess through. He owed her nothing at all. Lust, she told herself, did not make a relationship.

It was also harder for her because she wasn't worldly about these things, and was so inexperienced. She couldn't just discount what they had shared. Didn't want to believe it had been meaningless to him. Evidently it had been. And somehow she had to learn to accept that before she did something else stupid.

They climbed out of the car and Luc led her to a stairway. "I'm going to carry you," he said.

"Can't we take the elevator?"

"I don't have a key. Creed lives in the penthouse and it's a long climb."

She said nothing as, in a flash, he swung her onto his back. This time she kept her eyes open and saw little beyond a faintly colored blur. Her stomach felt as if she was zipping upward in a elevator that moved too fast.

In less time than she could believe, he set her on her feet again.

"Wow," she said. "That was a rush."

At that he favored her with a smile. "Like an amusement park ride?"

"Better." Far better, because for just a brief few moments in time she had been wrapped around him again. Damn, she wished she knew how to reach out to him, how to draw him closer. But he was already leading her down a short hallway to double doors, where he rapped.

The doors opened, revealing an auburn-haired man with eyes as gold as Incan treasure. Scent alone would have told Dani this must be Creed.

"Come in," he said and favored Dani with a warm smile. "Yvonne will join us in just a minute."

Creed's apartment astonished her. After what she had seen so far, the last thing she would have expected from a vampire was two walls made almost entirely of glass, punctuated only by a small kitchen area.

Bright colors were splashed everywhere, and the entire south and west of the city was visible from here. It took her breath away.

"This is some place you have," she said.

"I have an actual job that keeps me inside most of the night. I'd go stir-crazy looking at nothing but walls."

"Hi," said a light, cheerful voice from behind.

Dani turned to see a beautiful blonde dressed in

jeans and a sweater emerge from what appeared to be a bedroom.

"I'm Yvonne," she said. "You must be Dani."

She passed right by Luc to give Dani a hug. "Where are Jude and Terri?" she asked, turning to look at Luc.

"They went to the morgue. Terri has a plan to interrupt the birth of newborns."

"That's going to be dangerous."

"At least until dawn."

Yvonne brought out a plate of finger foods for herself and Dani, along with some hot chocolate. Creed brought out two bags of blood and for the first time Dani saw vampires eat.

She watched, swallowing hard, as bags of blood were emptied into tall glasses. Luc's gaze challenged her as he drank.

She made a point of staring while he took another drink, then reached for a cracker and cheese. He thought he was going to put her off because he drank blood? Not likely. The thought of it was evidently worse than the reality of it.

"Is that stuff any good?" she asked.

"You want some?"

Again that challenge. "Not my taste," she answered. "I just wondered about you guys."

"It suffices."

Yvonne gave her a friendly smile. "I think it was Terri who told me it's like the difference between champagne and rotgut wine."

"Eww." Dani wrinkled her nose.

"It serves its purpose," Luc answered.

"Apparently so. Still, it can't be easy."

"It's like being on a diet. That's all."

Creed looked about ready to laugh.

"What's so funny?" Dani asked him.

"You two remind me of agitated porcupines. Pull in your quills, both of you. We've got serious matters afoot."

Serious matters, indeed. Luc filled Creed and Yvonne in on the few things they didn't know, including the wolves who were supposed to meet them here.

"Lycanthropes? Here?" Creed looked astonished.

"You'll probably only meet my mother," Dani hastened to assure him. "I doubt she'd bring the whole pack up here."

"I'm sure she won't. This isn't the sort of place your pack would like, being so high."

She was surprised he knew that. "How much do you know about us? I mean them."

"Little enough. We try not to cross paths. Well, this is certainly a curious development."

Dani flushed. "It was all I could think of. There are only three of *you*."

"Oh, I'm not objecting. We need all the help we can get. I just never thought I'd see the day."

"The day is today," Luc said with a shrug. "They're out gathering intelligence right now. It would be nice not to be guessing what we'll face when we go after the rogues."

"Certainly. That always helps."

Then Luc looked at Dani and for the first time in hours she saw genuine concern on his face. "We have a problem, however. If the pack comes here after dawn, someone needs to meet them. And there is only one who can."

Dani lifted her chin. "Of course I'll meet them. Why is that a problem?"

"Because there will be no one to watch over you in the meantime, little wolf. No one at all."

"She should be safe," Creed objected. "My scent is all over this place, and the rogues have no reason to be interested in me yet."

"Ah," said Luc, "but now my scent is here, as well. And I have given them ample reason to loathe me."

Dani's fears clawed their way to the surface again, but she hoped they didn't show. Something in Luc's withdrawal, after he had been so kind to her, had stiffened her in some way. She was not going to lean on that damn vampire any more than she absolutely had to.

"If the rogues show up I can wake you, right?"

"Only if you have time."

"Well, what the hell do you want me to do about it, Luc? You can't stay awake, and someone has to be here to greet my mother and find out what the pack has learned, and that leaves me, the only person they'll trust. And you're forgetting something: the rogues can't run around after dawn, either. So what do you fear?"

He didn't answer and she knew she had him dead to rights. He still didn't look any less tense, though. Something was worrying him, most definitely.

Creed rose and reached for Yvonne's hand. "Dawn approaches. Don't be too long, Luc."

The two of them disappeared into the bedroom, closing the door quietly.

That left Luc and Dani utterly alone. Uncomfortable, she rose and went to stand before the huge windows, wrapping her arms around herself, seeking some kind of comfort. Not even if she strained could she tell that dawn was arriving.

"How do you know?" she asked finally.

"Know what?"

"That dawn is approaching? Or when to wake?"

"I don't know. I can tell the sun is about to rise because the back of my neck prickles with warning. It grows more pronounced the closer daybreak comes."

"And waking in those dark rooms?"

"Again, I don't know. Evidently we sense a rhythm to the days, conscious or not, visible or not."

"I see." Finally she turned to face him, because she had to know what was going on, no matter the price. "Luc, what's wrong? I get the feeling you hate me. Are you mad at me?"

He hesitated. "I certainly don't hate you, Dani.

And I'm not even angry now. But your pack has come. They'll take you home with them, as they should."

Her jaw dropped a little. "That's my decision, not theirs. And I can't go back. I don't belong there."

"But do you belong here?"

Her impulse was to respond that she did, but she smothered the words because she didn't know what was going on with him. Finally she settled on something reasonably safe. "I belong here now more than I belong there. I know that much."

He tilted his head, then faster than she could see he approached until he stood inches away. Reaching out, he lifted her crystal wolf's head necklace, moving it so that it caught and splintered the light into rainbows. As if he was pondering a mystery, or reminding himself of something. She wished she knew which. Then he lifted her chin with his finger so their gazes met.

"A long, long time ago, I was a fool and made a choice I regretted often. To save my own skin, which is sometimes not a very good reason, little wolf."

"Okay," she said quietly.

"I have seen the darkest parts of my nature. For a while I even reveled in them because I had neither the desire nor strength to fight them. I was a monster, Dani."

She felt her heart accelerating with dread. Did she want to know this? But she felt she had to. That he *needed* her to know.

"I was everything your pack taught you my kind are. *Everything.*"

"I guessed," she whispered. "When you talked of newborns."

"Obviously I was one of them."

"What happened?"

"Well, it was not all some wonderful revelation of conscience, although conscience began to play a role. It was also a need for self-preservation. Jude is quite right. If we don't control ourselves, we can't be safe. Humans will find a way to exterminate us. So again, the desire to save myself led me down a different path."

"I understand."

"You can't possibly understand. You've never faced such choices. You've never done such things. But at heart I am a monster. You need to know that."

She swallowed hard, but she wasn't feeling any fear. Instead, she was feeling an unexpected, strong sympathy.

"Then I met Natasha, my claimed mate. We lived together for just over fifty years and it was a joyous time, a joy I certainly didn't deserve."

"What happened?"

His face darkened and creased with pain. "There is nothing for a vampire that is quite like the wonder, the joy, the exquisite desire and satisfaction that comes from sharing intimacy with a human. It is not even the same with another vampire."

"Oh." Her heart tripped and then sped up, but for an entirely different reason.

His finger left her chin and ran down her throat to the pulse that raced there. "I can feel your desire for me. I can smell it. I feel the same, *ma belle.* The same and more."

She cleared her throat, struggling to keep her mind clear. "Natasha?" she reminded him.

"She thought to give me a gift. A great gift since I was true to her at all times. A demon enticed her and changed her back to human form."

Dani gasped.

"If you come into my world any further, little wolf, you'll find things you never dreamed existed." He sighed and took his finger from the pulse in her throat. She felt abandoned.

"Dani, I was horrified that she had done such a thing. I got angry, telling her that she was perfect for me as she had been, that I wanted no human, I just wanted her. And I was so angry she had made a deal with a demon. I couldn't imagine what she had bargained away to achieve this."

"Then?"

"She jumped from the window of our home, killing herself. She realized she had been seduced by a demon's promises and… I am not sure how much my reaction played into what she did. I blame myself."

"Oh, Luc, I'm so sorry!"

He shook his head. "It's done. There's more you need to understand. I had claimed her. For us that means something much more than love. When a vampire claims, it is beyond love and well into obsession. Had Natasha left me, I would have followed her to the ends of the earth. Instead, she left me by dying. Unfortunately that didn't end my obsession. I hunted the demon who had seduced her because my thirst for vengeance knew no bounds. I was, as Chloe told you the first night, insane."

"Did you get vengeance?"

"I thought so. But for nearly a year now I've been wandering from place to place, living only to choose the time and manner of my death. For if vengeance doesn't end a claiming, only death will."

Dani's heart seemed to be shattering. That he had loved Natasha that much overwhelmed her. He couldn't possibly have space in his life or heart for anything else. Hadn't he as much as said so? "Do you still want to die?"

"Oddly, little wolf, that desire has left me. Since I met you."

At that, everything inside her seemed to leap, even as some wise part of her brain reminded her that she didn't know enough yet to understand what she was getting into.

"I am not happy about this," he told her bluntly. "I do not want to care again, but care again I do. I told you we were playing with a fire you cannot imagine. What if I claim you, Dani? Will that content you or frighten you? Will I once again wind up wandering in search of my own death as I try to stay away from you? I don't know."

His eyes darkened. "I am quite sure, however, that you are not sure. So I will back away while we can still both escape."

Then he lifted his head. "It is time."

With that, he turned and disappeared into Creed's bedroom. This time the door closed firmly and she heard locks thud into place.

She stood frozen, her mind jumping in a dozen different directions at once as she tried to absorb everything he had told her. One thing she was sure about: he was warning her.

But warning her of what? That he might become obsessed with her? From what he had said, that was a pretty big deal, and it might be cruel of her to even flirt with the possibility. Did she really want Luc to be left insane or so desolate that only death offered him any hope of release?

No. Of course not. That would be cruel beyond bearing. So he was right, they had to keep a distance that left them both free. Except the thought of that distance, which she had barely tasted tonight, caused her a pain so deep she felt it to her very soul.

How could she have become attached so fast to a *vampire?* Maybe her mother was right. Maybe he had cast some spell over her.

But even as she considered it, she knew that wasn't true. Here he was, backing away to protect them both from an obsession he evidently wouldn't be able to control.

Trying to save her from himself and what he might become. To give her freedom to leave before he couldn't let her go.

It simply wasn't adding up. None of it. If he was worried about claiming her, then perhaps he was feeling the initial stirrings of the obsession.

If so, was there anything she could do to prevent it? Leaving him might not stop whatever was going on.

God, she wished she had someone to talk to who could explain.

Just then the door of the condo opened and Jude slipped in. "Made it just in time," he said with a smile. "Everything okay?"

"Yes. Terri?"

"She's safe. Any vampire who doesn't want to face the sun is going to ground now. Your pack?"

"I haven't heard."

He nodded and started for the door of the bedroom.

"Jude? A second?"

He paused. "I don't have many of them. Quickly."

"Why is Luc afraid of a claiming? How bad is it, really?"

"He's afraid because he did it once. Only he knows how much pain he experienced when Natasha died."

"But is it so much worse than love?"

"Yes." He faced her, eyes darkening. "We all try to avoid it, Dani. All of us. But sometimes it just happens."

"Why avoid it?"

"Consider. I have claimed Terri. If she were to leave me for any reason I would have two choices. I would either hound her to the ends of the earth no matter where she went, or I would have to die to set her free. Luc is right to be concerned. And if you care for him, heed that concern."

"So I should go back with my pack?"

"I didn't say that." He gave her a crooked smile. "I tried to avoid claiming Terri. It didn't work. And I'm the happiest vampire on the planet now. Just be very, very sure of what *you* want before you encourage him further. Good night."

He slipped a key card into the door of the bedroom and vanished inside. Once again she heard it lock.

She turned again and saw the very first faint lightening of the sky. Her heart ached, full of unhappy knowledge, but her body ached, as well. Staring out over the awakening city, she felt the ceaseless throb of desire for Luc, as if he had infected her somehow. He didn't even have to be there to make her want him with every fiber and cell.

Alone and disturbed, she watched the city brighten.

The day yawned before her endlessly.

* * *

It was nearly ten before Dani's mother arrived. She had to give permission to the doorman to let her come up, and was surprised when he acceded, apparently because it must be okay if she was in Creed's condo.

Lucinda arrived at the door a few minutes later and Dani let her in.

"Where are all the bloodsuckers?"

"Asleep. You know that, Mom."

"Yes." Lucinda, dressed in winter gear, dropped onto the couch. "Coffee?"

Dani felt a little like she was trespassing, but she went into the kitchen and made a pot. It was easy enough since Yvonne had left everything out, perhaps because she thought Dani might want it.

She brought two cups out to the living room and sat next to her mother on the couch. "The pack?"

"They're still out searching the streets. We've smelled a few vampires. Not that many yet. Less than a dozen so far. But we've also smelled something else. There are dead in some of the buildings, Dani. They haven't been discovered yet, and they may become newborns. We can't be sure."

"Did you note where they are? Terri's still at work. I can let her know where to look."

"What's she going to do about them?"

"She has a plan. She's the medical examiner. Did we tell you that? Anyway, she's insisting that the first step with each corpse that is brought to them is to remove the brain."

"Ah!" Lucinda's face lightened. "That's brilliant."

"At least until the rogues figure out what she's doing."

"They will, soon enough." Lucinda sighed and sipped more coffee. "We're tired, daughter. We're going to have to sleep for a while, but at least the vampires are sleeping, as well. And you. You look exhausted."

"I am. I've had my days and nights mixed up."

Lucinda's frown was faint, but evident to her daughter who had known her all her life. "So Terri is the wife of that one called Jude? Why hasn't he changed her?"

"He seems reluctant. He said something about not wanting her to go through what he's had to endure."

Lucinda thought about that. "You seem to have found an exceptional group of vampires."

"According to them, the rogues are the exception."

"Perhaps. Times have changed." Reaching out, she brushed Dani's hair back with a gentle touch. "I'm sorry we failed you."

"You didn't fail me. I failed the pack."

Lucinda shook her head firmly. "No. Never. It happens sometimes that one of us can't shift. That never made you any less in our eyes. But you weren't happy. I could see that. Are you happier now?"

Dani thought of Luc and the way he was pulling back. "I don't know. I thought I was."

"You need to be among your own kind. What I sense is that you feel you don't *have* a kind."

At that, Dani's throat tightened until it hurt. "Maybe not. I don't know yet."

Her mother gave her a quick hug. "Be careful, Dani. Don't let loneliness lead you astray. And right now, things are dangerous. I wish you weren't right in the middle of it all."

"I didn't put myself in the middle. I was attacked and Luc saved me. That's what put me in the middle."

"I'm grateful to Luc, much as it pains me." Lucinda's smile was crooked. "I sense he's very troubled, though. So be careful. Not just because he's a vampire."

Dani nodded. "It's okay. He wants to avoid me."

"Good." Something must have flickered over Dani's face because her mother suddenly looked concerned. "Dani, you haven't given him your heart!"

"No. No. Not that I'd have a chance to."

Lucinda pulled back a little. "I warned you, daughter. If you follow that path, you'll lose the pack."

"Did I ever *have* the pack?" The words burst out of Dani as anguish filled her. "Do you know what I am, Mom? I'm nothing. I'm not fully human, I'm not fully lycan, I'm not *anything!* I can't run in the moonlit woods with you. Heck, I can't run with the pack at all. At home I'm nothing but a pup sitter. Here I don't quite fit in because I know things humans choose not to know. I smell things they can't. I heal too fast. Well, I don't fit with the bloodsuckers, either. I'm just baggage right now. They're protecting me, nothing more. Do you know how that makes me feel?"

"Dani..."

"I know all the kind things you'll say to me, so don't bother. I know you love me. But you know something? Sometimes love isn't enough."

A few moments passed before Lucinda replied. "No, sometimes it's not. But to fully belong with *them*—" she nodded toward the closed bedroom door "—you'd have to become something we can't tolerate. Then what have you gained?"

"I didn't say I wanted to be one of them. I just wish there was somewhere I didn't feel like a burden. A place I felt useful."

"That's why you were studying nursing."

"After the last few days, I don't think that'll be enough anymore. I know things. I've seen things. I can't go back to pretending I'm just a normal, because I'm not."

"Then what do you intend to do?"

"I don't know. I honestly don't know." She looked down for a few seconds then drew a deep breath. "I have to find my way somehow. In the meantime, tell me where you smelled these corpses so I can let

Terri know. She can probably collect them all and deal with them before nightfall."

"And then what? Surely these rogues will figure it out."

"Luc and Jude thought that might actually be a good thing, because then we'll know where to look for them. If they come to the morgue, we'll be ready."

"We." Lucinda repeated the word thoughtfully, quietly. "All right," she said presently, switching to a brisk tone. "Give me some paper to write on. The pack will be there tonight, too."

Dani's heart squeezed again with fear. "Mom, you can all leave. I don't want any of you to get hurt."

"Do you honestly think we won't stand beside you in this? You know better, Dani. And if you choose to stand with those blood—your friends, then so will we. For now, at least."

Pack loyalty above all else, Dani thought as she went to the desk against one of the windows and found a pad and pen. She was still part of the pack, whether she felt like it or not.

Just then, she couldn't have said whether that was a good thing.

Just a few minutes later she called Terri and gave her the addresses. At least *some* newborns weren't going to awake that night.

Chapter 9

Dani slept most of the day after her mother left. She might as well have been drugged, so desperate was she for rest. The new schedule wasn't agreeing all that well with her biorhythms, she thought when she finally stirred to see the condo filling with the red light of a winter sunset. She felt as if she hadn't even rolled over on the couch, and she couldn't remember having dreamed.

For a few minutes she didn't move, looking up at the reddening ceiling, trying not to think about all the night might hold.

Somehow she suspected her new friends were going to try and keep her well and truly out of the fight. Heck, they'd probably try to lock her and Terri and Yvonne up right here.

Damned if she'd let them. Because as dead as she'd felt in sleep, she'd apparently reached a conclusion of some kind: if she didn't take a stand with her pack and the vampires, she would never again have a hope of not feeling like an utter failure.

Yawning, she rose, wishing for a hot shower, but instead she went to make coffee for Yvonne. And where was Terri? Fear prickled along her spine. Wasn't Terri supposed to return before darkfall?

Suddenly wide awake, she quickly filled the coffeemaker with grounds and water, and turned it on. Then she went to the bedroom door that was barred to her.

She hesitated, looking at it with loathing. It was a tangible reminder that she didn't belong here. She glanced over her shoulder at the sky, noting the sun had sunk below the horizon, leaving red streaks in low-hanging clouds. Was it safe to wake them now?

She didn't know. She just knew Terri wasn't here.

So she hammered as loudly as she could on the closed door. The thud sounded dull, and she wondered if it was even penetrating to the room beyond.

Desperate, she pulled out her cell and called the M.E. offices. A strange voice answered her. "I need to talk to Terri," she said, her voice tight.

"Dr. Messenger left a little while ago."

"Thanks." And she wasn't here yet.

She turned again to hammer on the door but before her fist made contact, it swung open and Luc slipped out.

"What's wrong?"

"Terri isn't back. I just talked to her office and they said she left a little while ago."

Luc scanned the sky. "Okay." He turned, throwing the door open. "Jude. Terri's not at the office and she's not here yet."

As if conjured by magic, Jude appeared, a phone in his hand. "Terri? Where the hell are you?" Then, "I'm on my way. I'll be there in a couple of minutes."

"I'll go with you," Luc said as Jude disconnected. "Is there trouble?"

"Not yet. She was late leaving. She's in her car, but that's no protection."

"I'll go," said a third voice. Creed appeared behind Jude and closed the door. "They don't know me yet and I can watch over the two of you from a distance. Luc, you stay here with the women. Yvonne's still asleep, and Dani needs protection."

Dani needs protection. Dani, for one, was getting awfully sick of hearing that, but she didn't know what she could offer right now. The vampires could get to Terri faster, and Dani's paltry efforts to protect the woman would amount to nothing next to them.

Jude and Creed departed immediately, leaving Luc and Dani alone in the living room as dusk deepened.

"Did anything happen?" Luc asked.

"As a matter of fact, yes. My pack found about ten corpses around town that hadn't been picked up. I called Terri and she was sending people out to get them. I suppose they've been debrained by now, or whatever it's called."

"Both good and bad news."

"Exactly."

She returned to the couch with her coffee, trying to appear nonchalant but certain she was failing. Just the sight of Luc now made her ache with longing, yet he seemed determined to keep as much space between them as possible.

Remembering what Jude had told her, she forced herself to look away. She had absolutely no right to risk putting Luc through the kind of pain Jude had talked about, that he himself had talked about. Certainly not when she wasn't sure of her own feelings.

Wanting him was not the same as loving him, and she had to keep that in mind. Unfortunately, she still remembered those minutes in the snow such a short time ago, minutes when she had found a transcendence she could never have imagined without experiencing it.

He'd ruined her, she thought. He'd evidently given her a taste for something she might never be able to experience again.

She swallowed a sigh and sipped coffee, pretending that nothing mattered. Pretending was something she'd had a lot of practice at. She'd been doing it her entire life, pretending things didn't matter, even when they hurt.

A phone rang and Luc pulled it out of his pocket. Dani rose and went to stand at the windows, staring out over the darkening city. She hoped Yvonne would get up soon. She needed something else to think about and maybe someone to talk to.

"You jest, *non?*" Luc said. "All right, but we could order food. Surely Creed has done enough of that."

A moment later he hung up, making a disgusted sound. "Terri wants to stop at the grocery. And they're letting her."

Dani turned around. "Sometimes we need to feel like we have *some* control."

Luc's brows lifted as he tucked his phone away again. "Is that what is wrong?"

"I didn't say anything was wrong."

"You hardly need to say it when I can smell distress all over you. Your muscles are coiled. I can see the heat in them."

She just shook her head and turned away.

"Talk to me."

"Why? You don't give a damn anyway."

"Ah."

In an instant she felt him standing behind her. His deep voice was little more than a breath in her ear. Despite her upset, she responded as she always did to him, with a warm quiver of passionate longing. "Is that what this is? I'm trying to protect you but you think I don't care? I told you that's not true."

"And I'm sick of being protected. All my life I've been tucked away in places so I would be safe. All except the months I lived here, at least until I was attacked."

"What is so bad about that? People only protect you if they care about you."

"I'm sick of feeling useless. Feeling like a failure. Like I don't belong anywhere."

"Now, *that* I can understand." His hands found her shoulders, gripping gently. "Perhaps you have just not yet found your world, Dani."

"I'm quite sure I haven't. I'm not a lycan and I'm not a human. And what do you see me as? A threat of some kind? Well, how can I possibly be a threat to anyone? I apparently can't even protect myself. Or help protect those I care about. If my mother had her way, I'd be back up north tending pups, and she'd take the car keys away because I couldn't… couldn't…" Her voice broke and she had to fight for control.

"You couldn't what?" he asked gently.

"I couldn't even run through the woods far enough to reach a road and hitchhike out of there. So I'd be a prisoner. And that's what you and the others are planning to do tonight, isn't it? Keep Yvonne, Terri and me prisoners while you and my pack go face the rogues. How the hell do you think that makes me feel, Luc?"

"Not good, I can tell."

"Someone attacked me and I couldn't even defend myself."

"*Four* someones," he reminded her.

But she wasn't listening. It was as if everything, every single thing in her life that had made her feel less valued, less important, less useful, was coming to a head.

"I was attacked," she repeated, "and I couldn't protect myself. I needed *you* for that. And now you and the others, including my pack, will be attacked and I'd just be a distraction, no help at all, so once again I have to stay in a cage and out of the way."

He turned her around and wrapped her in his arms, holding her close. She wanted to sag against him, drawn by his scent, by memories of what they had shared and by a desperate need for comfort.

"I understand," he said and ran his hand along her back as if petting her. The touch had a quite unintended effect, she was sure, as she seemed to liquefy and heat began to pour into her groin. But he was afraid of that, evidently with good reason. She forced herself to remain stiff.

"I've had a lot of time to ponder not belonging," he said. "We vampires don't seem to need it as much as your kind, probably for our own safety."

"My kind? Just what *is* my kind, Luc?"

"I don't know," he admitted. "But maybe you should find cause to rejoice in just being you, and stop worrying about things that make you different. So you are not fully lycan. So you are not fully human. These are not the best metrics to use."

"No? Then what is?"

"That you are loved. Love is what makes us belong. Love is what creates our place in the world. In all my centuries, I belonged only with Natasha.

I think the feeling you have is more common than you realize."

"Maybe. But what about being useless?"

"You compare yourself to things you are not when you define yourself as useless. We all have different contributions to make."

"Oh, that's so much crap!"

"It's not, little wolf."

"I told you not to call me that."

He sighed. "All right. Feel sorry for yourself. But you never know at what instant you may become the most important being on the earth for someone. Keep that in mind."

His words stung and she wanted to pull away even though she knew he was right. She was indulging in self-pity in the midst of a situation where her only concern should be the safety of those she cared about. And if keeping them safe meant staying locked up, then she should consider that the right thing to do.

"I'm sorry," she muttered finally.

"Don't be. I understand. On this, I understand. There was a day when I awoke out of the maddened haze of being a newborn and I realized I could never again be the man I had once been. I lost my friends, the remains of my family, everything I cared about. I would never belong with any of them again. I had become different."

"Yes," she admitted quietly.

"We had expectations of what our lives would

be, both of us. And in the end we were both disappointed, set apart. But I finally learned to stop loathing myself. Everything you say, Dani, speaks self-hatred. And for you, at least, none of it is your fault."

He tipped her head up and kissed her, long, hard and deep. Instantly she melted, her heart and body began to throb in time with his as if they were one. Stars whirled behind her eyelids, her entire being pulsed with need—then just as quickly he reappeared across the room.

"Luc…" Her head was still spinning.

"You tempt me, Dani. You tempt me in ways that make me concerned for my self-control."

"Then don't control yourself."

He made a smothered sound. "You don't know what you invite."

"Then tell me?"

"Already you crave me. Do you have any idea how *much* I could make you crave me? I could ruin you for anyone else. I could deprive you of any semblance of a normal life. Because of me you could spend the rest of your life hunting for another to give you the same experience. That is why I control myself. I will not harm you in such a way."

What in the world did he mean? Dani wondered, struggling against the yearnings he awoke, trying to find sense in his words. She had gotten the part about claiming being dangerous for him, but what was this about craving him so much that no one else would satisfy her?

But she knew. At some level she knew. He'd given her a taste of something the other night, and that taste was pushing her toward him despite all the warnings.

At this point, maybe she could live without him. Maybe not if they went any further. Already just thinking of never seeing him again caused a deeper pang than almost any she had known.

He pulled out his phone. "Jude, what's going on? Why aren't you back? Okay."

"Are they all right?" Dani asked as soon as he hung up.

His smile was crooked and a little wry. "I'm running on vampire time, expecting them to be back as fast as I could. Terri is still shopping. She says you all need a decent dinner."

"At the risk of her neck? Not likely."

"I have observed that when it comes to Terri, Jude would risk his life rather than deny her the least little thing she wants. And Creed is with them, keeping watch."

Dani tried to imagine such love, but came up short. Although she shouldn't, she reminded herself. Her family had come here and allied themselves with vampires because they loved her.

At once she felt small and ashamed. Before she could beat herself up any more, however, Yvonne emerged from the bedroom, freshly showered and dressed but looking weary and yawning.

"What's going on? Do I smell coffee?"

They gathered at the table, the two women with coffee, while Luc and Dani filled her in.

"Wow." Yvonne sighed. "I missed a lot. I wonder if I'm coming down with something. I don't usually sleep so long."

"Stress," Dani suggested. "I slept all day."

"Maybe. Life with vampires is seldom dull, I'll give them that." She yawned again and rubbed her eyes.

Dani looked at her. "How did you and Creed meet?"

"You'll never believe me."

"Try me."

Yvonne shrugged. "I went to Jude on the recommendation of a friend of mine who is a detective because there was some weird stuff going on in my condo. I met Creed there."

"You didn't have any trouble with him being a vampire?"

"I found it surprisingly easy to deal with, maybe because I write fantasy novels. I don't know. The biggest thing, most likely, was actually getting to know him."

"That makes a difference," Dani agreed. It had certainly made one for her. "I always knew vampires existed."

Yvonne nodded. "That's right. You're lycan."

"Not really, but my family is. And we always knew about vampires. So believing wasn't my problem. Getting over our…aversion to them was. Briefly."

"These guys are extraordinary," Yvonne said. She shook her head. "I have to admit I'm afraid. I've seen a little of what vampires are capable of. If they square off, all bets are off."

Luc said nothing. Dani looked at him, trying to read something on his face but failing. Her phone rang and she pulled it out. It was her mother, and she was on her way to visit them.

Almost at the same moment, the door opened and Terri, Jude and Creed entered with bags of groceries.

"Dinner," Terri announced brightly. "The three of us are going to have a feast."

"Make it four," Dani said. "My mother's on her way."

"We've got plenty. Am I feeding a wolf or a human?"

"Most likely she'll come in human form. Easier to get past security downstairs."

Terri laughed. "Very true."

Dani helped her and Yvonne set the table for four. The three vampires disappeared briefly into the bedroom, probably to have their own dinner in a place that wouldn't offend Lucinda's nose or sensibilities.

"It's snowing again," Lucinda announced as she arrived. She paused, looking Creed over, and frankly sniffing the air around him. Then Dani introduced her to Yvonne, and Lucinda joined them at the table for a meal of rotisserie chicken, potato salad and a green salad.

"The pack is out hunting again," Lucinda said while they ate. "Looking for more corpses. We were pretty thorough last night, but there'll probably be more soon. It's a big city, too." She paused, biting into a drumstick and chewing. "I left a watch at the morgue, to see if they'd home in on it as a problem. It's early yet, though. They might not have realized we got most of their monsters."

"Perhaps not," Luc agreed. "They have no interest in controlling the newborns that I can imagine, and sometimes it takes several nights for the change to complete."

Lucinda nodded. "And some may have already changed. So far we think we've identified ten vampires in town apart from you three."

"Only ten?" Dani felt immensely relieved.

"Ten is enough," Luc remarked. "They're not expecting us to have help from the lycans, though. My guess is once they have a sufficient number of newborns terrifying the city, they'll turn their attention to Jude. To me. Creed, you may still be off their radar."

He shook his head. "I wouldn't bet on it. I work with Jude a lot."

"I don't get it," Dani said. "If it's Jude they want,

why not just come after Jude? They can do the terrorizing part later."

Silence answered her. Clearly, Dani thought unhappily, vampires didn't read minds.

It was Lucinda who surprised them by answering. "If I were them, the first thing I'd want to do is prove Jude is an utter failure. That even though he's tried, he can't protect this city. He hasn't kept his own kind safe from notice."

"What good will that do?"

Jude answered. "It'll undermine vampires everywhere who follow the same rules."

"But you called for help from others like you. Why didn't they come? Don't they see how important this could be?"

"They now have to look to their own areas of concern. None of them believes there is only one group of rogues."

"Not exactly," Lucinda said, calmly continuing her meal.

"What do you mean, Mom?"

"Whether they believe there is more than one group of rogues is irrelevant. What did I teach you about the pack wars, Dani?"

"That territorialism made..." Her eyes widened and she looked at Luc, who sat with the other two a safe distance away on the couch. "They won't leave their own territories undefended. You *did* say vampires are territorial."

"Indeed." Luc nodded and looked at the other two.

They nodded, as well. "Perhaps even more than your kind."

"That's it," Dani said. "That explains it all. For the rogues it doesn't matter. They know no one will come to your aid. They can go after one city or territory at a time, the way the Wilani Pack did. I don't know what their eventual plans are, but Mom is right. They know you're not going to get any help."

Lucinda left after dinner, saying she wanted to check on her pack. She kissed Dani's cheek, promising to return before morning with any news.

Terri claimed exhaustion and disappeared into one of the bedrooms. "I worked most of the night and all day. If I don't get some rest I'll be useless."

Jude went with her down the hallway to another bedroom and returned a short while later looking quite content. The contentment didn't last long.

"We can't leave all the guard duty to the lycans," he said. "We need to take turns. I'll go out first."

Luc rose. "Not alone."

"Yes. Alone. I can call for help, but we have to divide up the work. Me first. You later. Give our newlyweds here some time together."

Yvonne blushed but Creed smiled. "I'll second that."

Soon he and Yvonne had disappeared into the main bedroom. Jude pulled on his long leather coat, but instead of going to the door of the condo, he headed for a sliding glass door that led out onto a terrace. Snow had begun to swirl thickly, catching the interior lights like jewels.

Luc followed him out. “Take care.”

“You know I will. You keep guard here. With any luck the wind will blow my scent away from the building.”

Then he disappeared over the ledge.

Luc stood outside for a while, hardly aware of the snow and certainly not aware of the cold.

Right now, for him, the bigger danger seemed to await him inside Creed’s condo: Dani.

He was drawn to her, dangerously drawn. She had awakened him in ways he thought would never be possible again. Every whiff of her scent aroused his hunger almost beyond control. She awoke the predator in him, the predator who wanted to take what it chose and damn the consequences.

He ached for her. He had told her he could make her crave him beyond her ability to manage, and he could, but he *already* craved her that way. Stepping back into that condo, filling his lungs with her enticing scent would test every bit of his self-control.

And being around her was fraying that self-control seriously. He tried to focus on the danger they were facing from the rogues, but powerful instincts kept pushing those thoughts aside. He wanted that woman. He wanted to seduce her, taste her, carry her with him to that pinnacle between life and death where bliss knew no limits.

His problem was that he knew exactly what that

was like. She didn't yet, and he had no business showing her. He had seen what became of humans who visited that place and then were abandoned by thoughtless vampires: they became addicts, always on a hunt for another fix, prey to the unscrupulous.

He didn't want to do that to her. And after Natasha and all he had endured since her death, he didn't know if he could offer any more than that.

He smiled with bitter amusement at himself. Before his change he hadn't much thought about anything. He'd been utterly absorbed in agrarian pursuits on his estates, pleasant enough to those he dealt with, but he wasn't sure he could ever remember suffering the pangs of conscience.

Well, why would he? Being born to a title and wealth had given him a certain level of arrogance; he knew which lines he dared not cross, and some that he was allowed to cross but never had. *Nothing* in his life had ever tested his conscience, although in retrospect he thought some of it should have.

So somewhere over the centuries, while living as a predator and pretty much using his wiles to get what he wanted, he had developed some kind of moral code. Amusing. Which brought him to this point in time. Fighting vampires to protect a rule he had accepted only reluctantly at first, and fighting himself to protect a human female from the consequences of ultimate pleasure.

Hell, it hadn't been so long ago that he'd carefully taken the blood he needed from willing women because it was the only way he could survive. Now he was reluctant to do even that, miserable as it was living on that stuff out of a bag, so full of preservatives.

But did all his reluctance arise from some moral code? He doubted it. He and Natasha had frequently drunk from the willing. They were easy enough to find at clubs that catered to human vampire fetishists. But since Natasha, he hadn't even done that.

Until he had held Dani in his arms in the snow and had been unable to prevent himself from taking a taste, a mere taste, of her lifeblood.

Even that little sip had been enough to intoxicate them both. He could see it in the way she looked at him, in the way she smelled sometimes. She wanted him. Oh, yes.

But he wouldn't give her what she wanted if it meant taking something too precious from her.

He couldn't.

He wondered if that would apply across the board now, or if it only applied to Dani. Troublesome question, one he had to find an answer to.

He sniffed the cold air again and found it clean. Jude's scent had vanished. If the rogues were abroad tonight, they were far away. Good.

At last he gathered his willpower around himself like a cloak and stepped back inside, only to be assailed by Dani's maddening, tempting scent. He closed the door and paused, looking around until he spied her curled up as small as she could get in a corner of the couch.

His heart quickened with need. Hunger pounded in his veins. He stood frozen.

"Did you smell something out there?" she asked, her voice small.

"No. Nothing."

"Then you were staying out there to avoid me."

He didn't know how to answer that. Nothing he could say would make things any better. Natasha had taught him that sometimes the only thing a man could do was say nothing at all.

Dani shook her head. Her chin quivered. "You didn't want to come in because of me," she repeated. "I'm driving you nuts."

He considered the word, then answered carefully. "That's an adequate description."

"Then go. Or I'll leave. This is making us both miserable."

"Both?" But of course he knew, although he doubted she could be anywhere near as miserable as he was. She had merely glimpsed the paradise he knew they could find together.

"Oh, don't equivocate with me, Luc. You say you want me and back away. You know I want you, and you still back away. It's not like there's some cosmic question here. Either you want me or you don't. If you really do, then my being here drives you nuts. You're certainly driving *me* nuts."

"Dani." He tried to make his voice stern, to put

all the command in it a vampire could manage, even though he'd suspected from the first that he couldn't vamp this one. "It can't happen. You don't seem to understand, and I don't know how to explain any better than I have already."

"Why should you care if I crave you for the rest of my life?"

Good question, some hungry portion of his mind answered.

"People survive broken hearts," she said, and her chin quivered again.

"Who is talking of hearts? We're talking of lust here. Desire. Passion. I want you, yes. I want you more than I've wanted anything in nearly forever. But you refuse to grasp the risks."

"You don't have to claim me."

"I might not have any choice!" He thundered the words and watched her curl up even tighter and hunch away from him. He expected Yvonne or Terri to come running out, but the condo remained still and silent.

He'd have given anything just then for some human intervention, but no rescue arrived. It was just him and Dani and the building electricity between them. Her scent filling his nostrils. His hunger pounding deafeningly in his veins.

The air was thick with things he knew too well and she couldn't understand at all.

"I'm sorry," she said brokenly, then leaped up from the couch to run to the back of the condo.

He should have let her go. But he was still a predator, whatever veneer he might choose to put on it, and seeing his prey flee unleashed an instinctive reaction.

He reached her before she had taken three steps, banding his arms around her like steel. He turned her toward him and she gaped up at him, real fear in her gaze. Ah, the fear. It intoxicated him as much as anything. The smell seeped from her pores, joining the electric desire that had dominated only moments ago.

He was losing it. Losing it bad. And he didn't know how to prevent what was about to happen.

He would not drink from her. Not one drop. He could satisfy some of her longing without crossing that threshold. Satisfy some of his need, as well. He knew of no other answer.

Bending his head, he took her open mouth in a kiss.

An instant later he felt her response, and triumph filled him.

She was his.

Chapter 10

He would be vulnerable. There was nothing as vulnerable as a vampire in the throes of passion, not even a sleeping one. Even if he didn't drink from her, he'd be so locked in the moment that he would notice nothing but the desire and Dani.

This was not the place or time, some still-sane part of him argued. All those exposed windows, two human women and another vampire who might emerge from their rooms at any moment…

Not the place. Not the time. But he couldn't seem to let go of Dani, couldn't seem to free himself from the miasma of desire long enough to think. He needed to think.

All he could think was that he needed to take

Dani somewhere. But he couldn't do that because he was guarding them all right now. He had a duty.

He swore as he tore his mouth from Dani's. "Not now," he said hoarsely. "Not now. Not safe."

With a supreme effort of will, he vaulted away from her and across the room. When he dared to look at her, her expression nearly crushed him.

She looked so forlorn, yet sleepy still from passion awakened. Disappointed. Abandoned.

Oh, he was so brilliant. All those feelings that tormented her about being not good enough had just been fed by his moment of thoughtlessness. He very nearly hated himself.

"It's not safe," he said again. "We have no privacy. Those windows wouldn't hold back a determined vampire. I'm on guard duty."

She gave a little nod, her eyes wide and wounded. And her chin quivered again.

He swore in French and turned his back.

Then, as if summoned by his frustration and worries both, Creed emerged from his bedroom. He paused on the threshold, tasting all the emotions in the air. He could probably read them as clearly as a letter.

Then he looked straight at Luc. "I'll take over now. Yvonne is feeling restless and wants to write. You two get some rest in the bedroom."

Luc had never before looked at Creed as the devil incarnate, but in that moment he very nearly did.

The temptation was almost more than he could bear, and he was sure Creed had figured it out.

But of course Creed had claimed a mortal woman. Why should he think it so bad if Luc did the same thing? He didn't know. Creed couldn't possibly know the agony of a claiming ended. He hadn't had to face it, so how could he truly perceive the dangers to both Dani and Luc in this craving?

Then he looked at Dani, read all her doubts, insecurities and fears, and knew that if he were damned eternally he couldn't leave her this way.

"Merci," he managed.

Yvonne followed Creed out. She seemed to sense the tension, looked at them in perplexity and said, "I'm sorry. Am I interrupting? I have a deadline and the ideas started flowing. I have to write, unless it'll cause problems."

Luc waved her grandly toward her desk, right next to Creed's in front of the windows. "Please, madam."

"I, um, changed the sheets for Dani," Yvonne said. Then she rubbed her eyes and headed for her desk.

Luc didn't say another word. He was past pretending a damn thing. In a flash, he scooped Dani up and carried her into the bedroom, kicking the door closed behind them.

He put her on the bed with reasonable gentleness then opened the small refrigerator Creed kept near the bed. He pulled out a bag of blood, extended his fangs and started drinking. And he made sure Dani could see.

But when he was done and had tossed the bag into the biohazard container he found no revulsion on Dani's face.

Well, that hadn't worked. Although he supposed it had been only a faint hope.

"Talk to me, Luc," she said quietly. "Just lie here and talk to me."

Lie with her and *talk?* He was quite certain he'd never heard a more ludicrous idea. "You jest."

"No, I'm serious. Obviously I'm tormenting you in ways I don't understand. And I can't say I'm exactly happy about it, either. So maybe we just need to talk."

"We've been talking. I keep getting the feeling you don't really hear."

"I hear. I get it."

"You couldn't possibly get it. I told you we were playing with fire. This is the kind of fire that could immolate one or both of us. That's the part you don't get."

"And we might all be dead in a few days if these rogues have their way."

That sounded logical, and that alone should have warned him he was utterly illogical right then. Moving cautiously now, he came to the bed and stretched out beside her. Her scent was heady enough that he didn't even need to touch her to set off a fresh storm of hunger.

If he had half the brain he'd always credited himself with, he'd put a hundred miles between himself and this tempting delicacy before he lost whatever was left of his soul.

She spoke tentatively. "So claiming is bad?"

"Only when it ends."

"And you don't want to risk that again."

"Most assuredly not." He sighed and rolled onto his side, judging that it was safe to just look at her. Face-to-face, but not touching. Safe, perhaps, but not wise. Those oddly colored eyes of hers still drew him, and he had to force himself not to look at the pulse he could hear throbbing in her neck. Finally, he settled on looking at her crystal wolf's head, a reminder of the gulf between them, of her insecurities—which he seemed to be doing his best to feed. *Hell.* "Most of us try to avoid it."

"But you can't control it?"

He shrugged. "I never had cause to think about it before. Natasha and I claimed one another and it was right for us. We thought we would have eternity together. We did not."

"You certainly wouldn't have eternity with me," she said, her voice dropping. "That much is obvious."

"Well, I could change that, but only if you wanted. And still, little wolf, there are no guarantees. Your family would disown you. Are you prepared for that?"

"I don't know."

He shrugged one shoulder. "So you see, it's better not to risk it."

"What will Creed and Jude do? They have human mates."

"The time will come when all their resistance to changing Yvonne and Terri will vanish for fear of losing them. Both of them have already said they want to change."

"I see." She closed those hypnotic eyes of hers and sighed. "Can I be honest?"

"But of course. I have been honest. I tell you of my darkest secrets, I make no lies about what I am—a predator who wants to make a meal of you. Someone who can take you to the stars and then leave you in despair for the rest of your days. I have told you of all the ways I could harm you. And your kind have at least taught you all that is worst in vampire nature."

Her eyes popped open and she glared at him. "Stop it. I judge you by what I see."

"And what you feel, which is seldom a good guide. I made you feel things I shouldn't have. I failed to maintain restraint."

"I didn't exactly help you, did I? I think I was at least half-responsible."

"But you don't know."

She scowled. "I'm not an idiot. I've heard all your warnings. But now I want to know the truth."

"I've been giving you nothing *but* truth. Truth about what?"

"I want to know what's wrong with me."

"Wrong with you?" He could scarcely believe his ears. "If there was something wrong with you, we wouldn't have this problem!"

"Shh," she said quickly. "You don't have to yell."

"I wasn't yelling. I'm stunned. You have brought me to my knees. I'm clawing for some vestige of self-control so that we don't both wind up hating me forever, and you think there's something wrong with *you?*"

"Is it because I'm lycan?"

"Mon dieu," he groaned.

"Well, you keep calling me *little wolf.*"

"An endearment. One that is special to you. It is not a curse, condemnation or complaint."

"Oh." Then she astounded him. The corners of her mouth lifted just a little, making her look almost impish. "So I don't revolt you. I bring you to your knees?"

"Most assuredly. Never in two centuries has anyone brought me so close to madness."

"No one has ever said anything so nice to me before."

More to astonish him. "Never? Are they blind?"

"Well, I'm not exactly attractive."

"Who told you that?"

"No one."

He suddenly caught on. "Because you never changed?"

She nodded.

"So…" he asked slowly, "no boyfriend ever?"

"No."

"No lover ever?"

"No."

"Mon dieu," he said again, this time in wonderment. Then conscience pierced him again. "I should not be your first. I cannot do that to you."

She bit her lip. "Luc…"

"Yes?" He hoped he sounded encouraging because he didn't want to wound this woman any more than he evidently already had.

"Luc, I don't know how…what… Do you want me to beg?"

That placed him squarely on the horns of a dilemma. To leave would wound her, however right that choice might be. To stay… He could do it, he decided. If he just didn't drink from her, it would be safe enough.

He could make her dizzy with pleasure without ever taking her to that place she would never forget. Surely he could maintain that much control.

"You don't have to beg," he murmured. "You don't have to know how or what. It will be my honor to show you the way."

A long shuddery sigh escaped her, her eyelids drooped, and she moved infinitesimally closer. Never in all his long, long years had he ever been offered something so precious as what he was being offered now.

Be careful, Luc, he warned himself. Then he gave up the battle.

* * *

Dani felt suspended in anticipation so intense that everything else flew from her mind. She hardly knew what had driven her to this point, what had caused her to make herself so vulnerable. She knew she wanted Luc; she knew she had never felt a longing so intense for anyone ever.

But she was equally certain she didn't exactly know what she was longing for. She had never made love with anyone, had never even come close. What if the only reason she was attracted to Luc was because he was the only person who had ever seemed to want her?

But that was a thought she didn't want to have now, not as his golden gaze passed over her from head to toe almost as if he could see through her clothing. The touch of his eyes had an almost physical impact, causing her to draw a sharp breath as if she needed more air than the universe could provide.

She suddenly wished she weren't wearing ordinary clothes but some sexy confection like the ones she'd often looked at in the stores but had never bought because there'd never been a reason.

But that didn't seem to be bothering Luc, she realized as she saw his gaze begin to darken. He leaned toward her and stole her breath once again with a kiss. When he lifted his head, he looked down at her from eyes gone completely black.

"You do indeed madden me, *ma chère.*" He sprinkled kisses on her face. "I am not sure I can restrain myself."

"Why should you?" Her voice sounded throaty and thick, hardly surprising since her entire body seemed to be filled with heavy, warm syrup. Her pulse now beat as strongly between her legs as it did in her heart.

"Because a woman's first time should not be rushed. I should take my time, opening you like the finest of wines, lingering over you for hours."

She caught her breath at the thought.

"However," he said, "with all that is going on, we might be interrupted at any moment."

Sad but true. Her heart hammered heavily, and her body felt on the brink of some amazing thing.

"Which risk do you want to take, *ma belle?* That I move too fast, or move too slow?"

Remembering their rough and ready near-mating in the snow, she didn't doubt for a moment that fast would be fine. Not the way she felt now.

"Just don't keep me waiting any longer." It was a whisper, hard to get past her lips. She felt so vulnerable, so frightened by this step, yet so eager.

A quiet laugh escaped him. "Then you shall see how fast a vampire can move, little wolf."

She didn't know what he meant until she felt her clothes disappear so fast that it was almost magic, so fast she barely had time to realize what he had done. The next thing she knew, he was lying beside her, naked, as well.

Naked and so very beautiful. Did being a vampire make them perfect? For perfect he appeared to her, his pale skin slightly ruddy, his muscles clearly defined. The kind of body that men spent hours in a gym to approach.

She caught her breath, looking him over with astonished but hungry eyes. No flaws. Not a one. How was that possible?

Then she realized he was looking at her in quite the same way, drinking her in with his eyes, and she blushed hotly, feeling it all the way to her toes.

He smiled. "That blush drives me mad." Reaching out, he caught both her wrists then held them with one hand above her head. She felt exposed and helpless in the most delicious way, and the throbbing between her legs grew until she felt little else.

Until he touched her, tracing her cheek, then her neck with his fingers. Ripples of delight ran through her and she closed her eyes. His fingertips paused at the pulse beating in her throat.

"That," he said huskily, "calls to me in ways you cannot imagine. Your pulsebeat. The sound of your heart pounding. The flow of the warm blood in your veins. Ah, you feel so warm, you smell like a garden of delights."

She shivered with pleasure as his touch trailed lower, finding the peak of one breast. He touched her there gently, brushing back and forth until she nearly cried out for something harder, stronger, needing more than she knew how to describe.

"You blossom for me," he murmured, then followed his fingers with his mouth, sucking her nipple, gently at first, then harder.

She gasped, arching toward him, wanting to clutch his head for fear he would stop, but he still held her wrists prisoner.

Each pull of his mouth was echoed with a throb between her legs, and she felt herself grow damp with need. Every nerve ending sizzled in time to her body's demand for more, and more.

He obliged her. His mouth remained fastened to her breast, first one and then the other, as his fingers traced light circles that moved ever lower, across her midriff, approaching that nest that no one had ever touched before.

Another gasp escaped her as he nipped her nipple, not hard, just enough to sting a bit. Pain turned instantly to a conflagration of pleasure.

Beyond thought, now a bundle of needs she didn't fully understand, she twisted toward him, throwing one of her legs over him, opening herself to any touch he chose to give her.

His gasp further enflamed her, and she tried to press even closer, but then his fingers plunged between her legs, stroking her most delicate flesh.

At first the touch seemed almost too painful to bear. An instant of shock nearly threw her out of the moment, but then the surprising pain transmuted, becoming at once pain and ecstasy, pulling her further upward into a place she had found only once, and not like this.

Everything was more intense, more exquisite, this time without any clothing as a barrier. The merest touch of his breath, his hands, his mouth… every whisper across her skin felt like a match being struck.

The moisture between her legs eased the path of his stroking fingers. She felt him slip one inside her, then cup her tightly until she moaned and rubbed herself against him.

He released her wrists at last and she tried to find him with her own hands, her own mouth, needing to share all that she was feeling. One hand found his rigid staff, the other pulled his face to her neck.

She needed more, so much more. She wanted him to drink from her again, too, to take her to that place where she hadn't been able to tell them apart.

Instead, he pulled his head back just a little, silently refusing her request. But he denied her nothing else. With his hands and mouth he taught her her body's secrets. He lifted her to a high pinnacle until fear joined passion as she wondered if she would ever reach the summit.

The ache in her was so hard it almost hurt, yet it pulled her along, undeniable.

She needed…she needed…

Then between one instant and the next she exploded. Her body spasmed so strongly that she went rigid and helpless.

His relentless fingers never stopped. When he slid down and captured her clitoris with his teeth and tongue, she thought she would die from the pleasure and pain of it. With licks and nips, he taught her that this was a summit she could reach more than once.

Until at last she lay exhausted and spent, surrounded by the cool arms and legs of a vampire.

She couldn't even move. Nor did she want to. His hands trailed over her gently, almost soothingly, bringing her back to earth.

"How do you feel?" he asked softly.

"Amazing," she admitted. Then she felt a pang. "But what about you?"

"I drank from you the other night. For me it was as if I were you."

Her heavy-lidded eyes opened at that. "Still?"

"Still."

"I wish…"

He stopped her with a finger over her lips. "Don't wish it. Please. Don't even ask that of me."

So she swallowed the plea, and at least for now admitted he was right. For now. She couldn't risk causing him any more pain unless they were both certain of what they wanted, and while she was growing increasingly convinced, she was sure he was not. He didn't want to risk another claiming, and who was she to put him in a place where he might, unless she was positive she wanted him forever?

Just thinking of forever brought back memories of

her pack. They would never forgive her. Her mother might, but Lucinda was right: the rest of the pack might not be able to accept such a thing.

But she didn't want to think about that right now. She didn't want to think about anything except how marvelous she felt, and how good it felt to be lying with Luc like this.

As if circumstances would allow that.

There was a knock on the door. In the blink of an eye, she found herself covered to her chin beneath blankets. She looked around, startled, and saw a quick blur as Luc dressed.

In less than five seconds, he was answering the door. She heard Creed say, "Jude wants to take the women to the cabin. The rogues are starting to circle in around the morgue."

"All right. When?"

"He wants me to take them as soon as possible. I don't know if I'll be able to get back before dawn."

"Best, perhaps, if you stay with the ladies."

"Yes. But you need help here."

"I think we can handle it with the assistance of Dani's pack. The important thing is for the two of you to protect your ladies."

He closed the door and reappeared, sitting on the bed beside Dani. "You must prepare to go, *ma belle.*"

"No."

He arched one brow. "No?"

She shook her head. "You need me to ensure my

pack doesn't consider you two a threat. If I disappear, there's no telling how they'll react."

"I don't want you exposed to this danger."

"I've already been exposed to it, and right now I have a score to settle." She supposed he could smell the fear that was seeping into her body, but she wasn't going to let him use it against her. Nor was she going to let it rule her. She knew her pack. She knew how deep their loathing for vampires ran. If she simply disappeared, no explanation would be enough.

"Tell Creed to take Yvonne and Terri. I'm staying."

"Dani..."

She shook her head, hoping she looked as determined as she felt, despite the fear that had begun to course through her.

"I could not bear losing you, little wolf."

"My pack will protect me. The question is whether they'll protect the two of you."

And that really *was* the question. Scared or not, she knew with absolute certainty that she would never forgive herself if her pack turned on Luc. Never. And there was only one way to guarantee they wouldn't.

She also had a score to settle. She hadn't allowed herself to think much about the attack on her, having chosen instead to bury it at the back of her mind to deal with when the threat was gone. But she realized that in one other way she was truly lycan: *nobody* was going to get away with nearly killing her.

She lifted her chin and stared straight into Luc's eyes. They had darkened again, no longer the beautiful golden color, but instead they had become windows on the night.

"I must go with you," she repeated. "I'm the only one who can protect you from my pack. I'm the only one who can make sure you don't have to kill one of my family to save yourself. Do you think I could live with either outcome?"

At that he sighed. "Sometimes I am not so fond of logic."

"It's true, though."

"I cannot deny it."

Rising, he went back to the door. "Creed, Dani is staying. Just take Terri and Yvonne. Keep guard on them along with Chloe."

Then he closed the door and faced her, his expression grim. "You had better dress, little wolf. And dress warmly. Now it begins."

Chapter 11

Before she and Luc left Creed's for the morgue, Dani got in touch with her mother.

"We're in human form right now," Lucinda said, "but the others seem to be circling in on the morgue. Your friend Terri is gone, right?"

"Creed's taking her and his wife up north right now."

"Why didn't you go?"

"Mom, can you honestly promise me that the pack wouldn't turn on Luc and Jude?"

A few beats passed, then, "No. I can't. I can try, but if we get into a fight the blood lust will rise. They might not distinguish."

"They will if I'm there to stand between them."

"Ah, Dani! They might hurt you, too."

"I stand a good chance. I'm part of the pack."

"And you smell like vampire!"

"I'm still their sister and cousin. And you're the alpha. But it might take both of us to protect two vampires."

Lucinda sighed. "You were always too brave."

"It's part of being lycan, Mom."

Finally her mother laughed unhappily. "Stay close. Remember, the pack works together."

"I remember."

When she put the phone deep into her jacket pocket, Luc reached for her hand. "Tonight we fly across the rooftops, little wolf. And I think your mother isn't happy."

"She isn't. No one's happy right now. Where do we meet Jude?"

"Not too far from the morgue. He's found a place from which he can keep watch. The danger lies in getting there without being spotted. They can see me no matter how fast I move and if they found the one I killed they surely have my scent. We must try to make it look like I am taking you to feed on you."

"How do we do that?"

"You're going to have a very uncomfortable ride any time I smell a threat. Your family?"

"They're in human form right now, keeping an eye out."

"They can't protect themselves in human form."

"They can shift swiftly and will. They can smell a vampire as far away as you can. Maybe farther."

"I would believe farther," he admitted. "There is surely a purpose to a nose so long."

A laugh escaped her, and she thought he was probably right.

He put her on his back again, with her arms around his neck and her ankles locked around his hips. They stepped out onto Creed's terrace and then the amazing began.

With a single leap that left Dani blind because of the cold, cutting wind caused by his speed, they landed on the next rooftop. He paused a moment to sniff the air and let her get her bearings, and then they were off again.

She barely had time to register when they landed before they once again leaped. On the occasions when he gave her a chance to see where they were, she marveled at the distance they had covered.

At one point he settled her into a corner on a roof, surrounded by a chest-high parapet, and vaulted himself up onto the top of the barrier to taste the air. She could hear him drawing deep breaths through his nose and exhaling them through his mouth.

Then he was crouched beside her again. "We're getting close. I can smell another of my kind and I don't recognize the scent. Oddly, it's not one I tasted on the air the night I met you."

"A new ally? Or a newborn?"

"I'm not sure. The smell is not so different unless the newborn is blood drenched. So far I don't detect any blood in the air."

She nodded and swallowed. The brave words she'd spoken only a little while ago now sounded foolhardy. But then her spine stiffened. She *did* want payback, the lycan part of her admitted. She craved it. And then there was Luc, as well. However strong he might be, however well he might be able to stand up to a vampire, the pack had a true advantage in numbers, and their strength was huge.

"We need to keep this fight on the ground," Luc muttered.

"What do you mean?"

"Only that your pack can't be of much help if we carry the battle up to the rooftops."

"How can we prevent that?"

"I'm thinking. I suspect Jude and I may have to expend a lot of our efforts to keep these rogues from climbing walls once they know your pack is involved."

"I wish we could move it to the countryside. They'd have far less advantage out there."

"Ah, but the attacker always has the advantage of choosing the place."

"Unless we can lure them somehow."

She saw him nod slowly, clearly thinking about it. "Perhaps into the morgue, if we can get the humans out."

"Some plan, huh?"

He smiled at her and cupped her cheek briefly. "We've known from the start we might not be able to choose our ground. In that, they've always held an advantage."

He stood up, sniffing the night again. "Let's go."

He reached for her, then paused. "I think I had better start carrying you over my shoulder. It won't be comfortable, but it will create an impression that I'm abducting you if anyone sees. I will try not to jar you too much. And you can watch my back."

"If I can see anything," she said a little drily. She was glad she had managed to sound so casual when she was beginning to feel icy fingers of fear clawing inside her. Surely she had to be nuts. Everyone wanted her out of this, and she had put herself dead center. But once again even a moment's reflection reminded her of her reasons. They would just have to trump her fear. They *had* to.

With the padding of her winter parka, the ride wasn't as bad as she anticipated. And Luc seemed to make an effort to keep his stride even and to land softly when he leaped.

As for watching his back, most of the time the world was receding too quickly, although she found that if she could focus on one thing, it became clearer.

Then he stopped again, tucking her into a corner between some vents that rose above roof level. "We're here," he murmured close to her ear.

For the first time she realized the wind had picked up. It was not all Luc's speed, and snow crystals stung her exposed cheeks where they could find them.

"You can't smell anything," she said. "The wind."

"Only from one direction. Let's get inside quickly. So far I don't think we've been spotted."

He lifted her again, carried her to a roof access door and let them inside.

At once she smelled the musty staleness of an abandoned building. Even the cold couldn't stifle the odors of a place that was probably rotting from the inside out. It was also pitch-dark. Which didn't bother Luc in the least. What amazed her was how fast he could take the stairs without a light to guide him.

Then they emerged into a room and he set her on her feet.

Tall, filthy windows let in some light from the surrounding city and she saw Jude, unmistakable in his long leather coat, over by one of them.

"Anything?" he asked.

"The wind has picked up. I smelled someone at a distance briefly, but now I am getting scents from only one direction."

"They suffer with the same limitations."

"Have *you* seen anything?"

"No. I caught wind of them back when I called you. I circled around and got the sense they were gathering, but nothing since." He looked at Dani. "You shouldn't be here. But since you are, have you talked with your mother?"

"They're out searching the streets. I can try to check again, but if she's shifted to wolf, she won't answer."

"I understand. Just try. We need some intelligence before they attack the morgue. At least I assume that's their plan, since their newborns aren't emerging from the place."

"Maybe," Luc suggested, "they're expecting some of them to emerge tonight."

"Possible, I guess. But why gather? They don't want to control them. At least I presume not."

Dani had pulled out her phone and now called her mother. "Any news?" she asked. "We're here near the morgue."

"We're getting some mixed information. They began gathering, but some seem to be dispersing. Maybe eight or ten of them right now."

Dani passed the information to Jude.

Luc stiffened. "Do you suppose they have realized the newborns aren't there? And that neither is your wife? They might be hunting up near your office."

"Mom? Can you track them?"

"Do you need to ask, Dani?" Her voice was gently chiding. "I'll tell the others, but I think they've decided on something else. I'll let you know the instant we learn anything."

"Thanks, Mom."

She looked at her companions. "My pack is going to try to track them. But where would they have gone?"

"The damn problem here," Jude said, "is we don't know how much they know about *us.* We know they're after me, personally, they might know Luc's involved or maybe not. If they know much about me, they probably know that Creed has been a friend for years and sometimes works with me. What if they go after Creed first?"

"Well, he's not there."

"Of course not. But if it's him they're after..." Jude fell silent. "They could know a lot about him, too. Just knowing who we are feeds them information, while we have no handle on who exactly they are. And even if we did, they're on the move. They have no hindrances, no humans to worry about. We can't pin them down."

"My pack can," Dani said. "If only they would gather somewhere away from tall buildings."

Jude straightened. "I'm going to take a sniff outside. Wait here."

Luc stopped him. "I think I have a plan."

"Probably the same one I do. Just let me check first. I don't want the people working in the morgue to become victims."

Jude turned into an almost invisible streak of black in the dark room and vanished.

"What's your plan?" Dani asked.

"You said something about luring them. It caused me to think. We can lure them out of town. It may be they don't especially want their reign of terror before they get rid of Jude and possibly the rest of us. Perhaps they were relying on the newborns for most of that. It is impossible to know."

"Yes."

"But since they want Jude and most likely are able to calculate that he might be behind what happened to the newborns...well, it is as Jude said. They know who he is and could learn a lot about him, including his relationship with Terri. So they gather here, find there are no newborns, few if any have been born elsewhere, but they can also tell easily enough that Terri isn't there."

"Yes, I found out just by asking."

"Exactly. So they would then next move to Jude's office. Nothing there. And if they know of Creed, then they would go there next. But what if they have been able to learn that Creed owns that cabin?"

"Oh, my God! But how would they find out?"

"I don't know. Property records?"

"But most of those offices close shortly after dark."

"They wouldn't need the offices to be open. You forget, most property records are online now."

Fear now clawed its way right up Dani's throat. "We can't wait."

"We can't act until we know *something*. If they don't know about the cabin, we don't want to lead them there. We need some indication of where they are going."

In a burst of frustration, Dani said, "This is impossible!"

Luc once again cupped her cheek briefly. "*Ma belle,* very little is impossible. This is annoying and troublesome, yes, but sooner or later to accomplish their goal of killing Jude, they will have to emerge. That much is certain. They are flouting his rules with their killings, but it may be they are not ready to begin the reign of terror I feared. Certainly there may not be enough of them, especially without the newborns. So…" He shrugged in that French way. "We know their objective, which leaves us less than blind."

"*Slightly* less than blind." Her phone rang and she tugged it out of her pocket just as she felt the wind of Jude's return. By the time she opened her phone he was standing over by the window again.

"Yes?"

Lucinda's voice poured into her ear. "They have passed Jude's office and are now moving in the direction of Creed's. Definitely a northward movement. Ask your bloodsucker friends if they might be able to follow Creed from his building. I gather he took the women in a car."

Dani asked the two of them.

"He would have taken a car," Luc answered promptly. "He could not carry them both that distance without them suffering too much from the cold."

"And yes," Jude said quietly, "they would be able to follow the fresh scent of the exhaust. Once they detect his departure with the women, they would move on. They might well know he owns the cabin."

"Dawn grows nearer," Luc reminded him. "Would they risk being in the open to try to follow? It is my guess they will not. So possibly we can corner them in the next two hours, or we will have to wait for tomorrow night."

He looked at Dani and nodded.

"We're going to try to corner them at Creed's," she said into the phone. "In the parking garage, I assume, because if they go to his condo they'll find him gone."

"There's one advantage to that," Luc said as he swung her up onto his back. "If we can keep them in the garage, they won't have anywhere to run."

Almost before she knew it, Dani stood on a rooftop several blocks away from Creed's. Even at this distance she could identify his balcony and see that there was movement on it. Evidently Luc's eyes were even better.

"They're there," he said. And just as he spoke, snow began to fall. "We need to meet with your mother. Plan. Now."

So Dani pulled out her phone again. There was no answer this time, and she felt her heart sink. "They must have shifted." She clenched her mittened hands and wondered whether she was cold from the winter night or from fear.

But a few minutes later, her phone rang. It was

Lucinda. "Do you know how hard it is to answer a phone that I'm wearing on a collar?"

"Sorry, but Luc says we need to plan. There are some vamps on Creed's balcony right now."

"Put that bloodsucker on with me."

She passed the phone to Luc. He took it as if it might explode. "Hello?"

Dani listened, wishing she could hear both sides of the conversation.

"We're downwind, they can't smell us," Luc said. "Your smell is not that distinct from other canids, so no. They shouldn't suspect. We're mortal enemies, after all."

He listened, nodding slightly. "All right. I doubt they'll come down the stairs, but regardless of which way they go to check the garage, once they've entered it, getting back through the security doors or elevator will be impossible without a key. I'll get closer and let you know."

He passed the phone back to Dani. "Mom?"

"We're going to set a guard at the base of the building. What we need to know is when those bloodsuckers go into the garage and can't get out except by way of the entrance and exit. Luc is going to watch and let us know. Give him your phone so he can keep in touch with me."

"I'm not staying here alone! And I'm not letting him go alone."

"I know his scent. We'll protect him. You stay safely away."

"Damn it!" Dani swore as she closed the phone. "I guess I'm just baggage to be carried around. I need to be there."

Luc looked at her almost ruefully. "If I take you over there, your mother will shred me. Is that what you want?"

"No, but…there has to be something I can do!"

Luc and Jude exchanged looks. Jude sighed. "She's your problem, my friend. But I've found it can be costly to deny a woman what she wants."

"Ah, you are so helpful," Luc replied sarcastically. He looked again at Dani. "So you don't care if I get shredded by your pack for exposing you?"

"I care if you get shredded by my pack because I'm not there. Even my mother admitted that if they get into a fight and the blood lust rises, they may attack you and Jude."

"Lovely," remarked Jude from where he leaned against a parapet.

"I *have* to be there," Dani insisted.

"It's not just my safety that concerns you, is it, little wolf?" Luc's voice had turned gentle again.

She flushed and hoped he couldn't see it. Although the damn vampire could probably smell it.

"I understand," he said after a moment. "All of us sooner or later must prove something to ourselves. The problem I am facing…"

Jude cut him off. "While you two discuss this, I'll just go see what's going on at Creed's, why don't I?"

Luc swung toward him. "They know your scent."

"We assume they do. But with all the comings and goings of vampires lately from my office, they may not. Yours could be equally identifiable. Just let me go keep a watch. I'll stay downwind and get back to you shortly. In the meantime you can settle your, ah, differences. Need I remind you that dawn isn't that far away?"

Then he was gone.

Luc turned his attention back to Dani. "I understand," he said again. "I do. But what I question is how you can help, other than to protect me against your pack. You surely haven't forgotten what those vampires did to you."

"No. I haven't." The memory, when she allowed herself to touch upon it, was still fresh, raw and painful. How helpless she had felt, how overwhelmed. How terrified.

"You fought them once, Dani. You don't need to fight them again."

"But I do. I have to be able to live with myself, and frankly, Luc, that hasn't been terribly easy at any point in my life since childhood."

He turned and looked out over the city. "I am thinking," he said, "that Terri's plan to stop the newborns before they could emerge has changed the rogues' direction. They will not be able to wreak their reign of terror and watch Jude be undermined before they kill him. No, they have realized that he is at least part of what is standing in their way yet again. They have focused on eliminating him. *Then* they will play their ugly games with this city in complete freedom."

"And this means?"

"I guess you will get your chance, Dani. To prove yourself. Because we are going to have to try to take them in the garage."

"Are you sure they'll even go there?"

"They'll smell all of us in Creed's condo. When they find no one, the next obvious step is to see if we departed by car. They'll note the smell of a car having left recently. They'll decide to follow it. They want to know where we are."

"Assuming they don't want their reign of terror first."

"I think Terri and your pack ended that. Between your pack finding all those bodies, and Terri making sure the brains were removed, I doubt they have increased their numbers. Certainly not numbers that are under control. If one or two newborns slipped by, they can't do much in a single night. I think now they know Jude is onto them, and they'll want to get him and the rest of us out of the way first. It is what I would do."

There was something so hard in his gaze just then that she shivered. For an instant she felt her pack's primitive loathing of vampires, and then she remembered this was Luc. The loathing vanished at the reminder. Luc had saved her life. Luc had become her lover in such an incredible way, and when she had lain defenseless with him he had done not one thing to harm her.

"How can I help?" she asked.

"Indirectly," he said. He pulled the phone Jude had given him out of his pocket. "Are they still at the condo?"

He listened then said, "Good. I'm going into the garage. I'm going to leave my scent and Dani's. And yours, if you'll part with your coat for a while. Then I'm going to lay a trail."

He hung up.

Dani stared at him, aghast. "You can't go in there alone!"

"Just briefly. Call your mother and tell her what I am going to do. I'm tired of trying to second-guess these rogues. I'm going to make sure that tomorrow night they head north. We'll get ready to meet them along the road. Give me your jacket."

Numbly she obeyed, handing it over. He passed her his own and wrapped her in it, taking care to ensure she was fully enveloped. Then he cupped her cheeks and kissed her lightly.

"When this is over, *ma belle,* we have something to discuss. But right now, we must push this to an end. Call your mother. Tell her I am setting a trail. Ask her to make sure it is followed. Then we'll all be going to ground for the day. Somewhere."

Then he was gone. Dani stood frozen for a split second, terrified out of her mind that something would happen to him. Then a thought pierced her terror and reminded her of the one thing she could do to help him. She picked up her phone and dialed.

"Mom? Mom, Luc is going into the garage to lay a trail. He's going to make it look as if all of us headed north. He wants you to keep watch to make sure they follow."

"I thought we were taking them in the garage?"

"Apparently he feels there's not enough of the night left to do it. Or something. Anyway, he seems to have become determined to take them north of the city somewhere along the road."

Lucinda was silent for a moment. "That's a better plan," she agreed. "I doubt all these vampires would allow themselves to be caught in an enclosed space at the same time. But in open country, it's different. And they're not aware of *us*. We can round them up like chickens."

"Maybe that's the idea."

"This Luc of yours is smart. All right, we'll keep watch and make sure the rogues follow the trail. Don't call me again unless it's urgent. These damn bloodsuckers can probably hear my phone vibrate from several blocks away."

"Okay. I love you."

"I love you, too, sweetie. I'm just sorry you were never sure of it."

Then her mother was gone. Dani shoved her cell into the pocket of her jeans and gathered Luc's jacket around herself. It smelled of him. Amazing how good that smell had become to her when only a few days ago the scent of a vampire, any vampire, had set her nerves on edge.

Jude was the first to return. Just about the time Dani felt she would need to scream to release her fear and tension, Jude rejoined her, clad only in his shirt and slacks.

"Aren't you freezing?" she asked blankly.

"I don't feel the cold. Luc succeeded. He left all our scents in the garage and headed north."

"God, I hope he can move fast enough."

"He's ahead of them, moving at top speed. They won't be able to catch up. The problem is that he'll have to circle back or find someplace to go to ground. But then, so will they. Your pack is following at a safe distance behind the rogues."

It was odd, Luc thought as he sped northward out of the city. Just a few short days ago, his primary concern had been choosing the hour and manner of his death. Now that he could die at any moment simply by slowing down, he no longer wanted to die.

He blamed Dani for that. Yes, blamed her. Death was an easy release, but hanging around because of one human female was far from easy. He no longer felt he might be betraying Natasha. Indeed, those feelings had vanished last year when he had joined Jude and Creed in sending back to hell the demon that had deluded Natasha.

But cherishing her memory had become an obsession, one that had been driving him steadily toward death. And now he was free of that obsession, and ironically at the moment he was in the most danger of dying.

The thing that struck him as he carried the two jackets with him, leaving a trail as clear as a lit causeway to his followers, was that his decision to get involved in this had not been driven by concern for the human species, concern for Jude or concern for himself. It had been driven by concern for Dani.

He had looked into those silvery-blue eyes of hers the first time and had been captivated. And regardless of the arguments he had made about why he was involving himself, the one he had not acknowledged was the most important of all: he didn't want Dani to live in the kind of world these rogues wanted to create.

Live or die, he didn't care so much for himself. He cared for Dani's sake.

A fine fix.

And his concern for Dani's future had only continued to grow. Thinking about it as he raced north, it occurred to him that the best thing for her might be for him not to survive this mess. Then she would be utterly free to choose her path.

Except Dani didn't seem all that happy with her path. She regretted not being able to shift like the rest of her family. She more than regretted it. It had gutted her in some very important ways. It hurt him to see those moments when she utterly lost her self-confidence.

A mile out of town, when buildings had thinned almost to nothing, he stopped. The back of his neck prickled almost hotly with warning of the coming dawn. He had to get to ground soon. But so did they. He was willing to bet that they wouldn't come out from the security of dark places with the remnants of night shrinking so rapidly. They knew they couldn't catch him. Tracking him would have to wait until tomorrow night.

Looking around, he noted a grove of trees. At once he dashed toward it, trailing Jude's coat in the snow here and there. In the grove, he patted some of the trees with his hand and with the jackets, then he darted north again.

Time was running out. Turning east, he ran a circle out into the fields and entered the city from a different direction. At least now they should have a reasonably predictable path to watch at nightfall.

Back in the city, he slowed down a bit, pulling out the phone Jude had given him. "I'm back. Where should we meet?"

"Damn good question," Jude said. "They followed your path north. I still haven't heard back from Lucinda, and I'm not sure they won't resort to checking my place or Creed's again."

"We've got to go somewhere."

"My place," Jude said finally. "I haven't been there in so long they must have decided I've gone to ground."

"Well, I left a trail from Creed's place out into the

countryside. And they've got to go to ground just like we do. Dani's pack might even be able to tell us where. It would give us a starting point."

"All right. My place. I'll get Dani there safely."

"Thanks, Jude."

"My pleasure. You just get there safely, as well. Look out, these guys probably have more time to prowl than you do."

Luc wasn't sure what Jude meant by that, except perhaps their secure places for the daytime hours might be nearer to them than he was to Jude's office. When he thought about it, he decided Jude could be right. If they were at all wise, they'd have any number of deep basements they could retreat to around the city.

He'd resorted to some of them himself.

So instead of running faster than the wind in a direct beeline, he climbed to the rooftops and took frequent pauses to test the air. He was still carrying the coats. Maybe he should have ditched them somewhere.

He paused again and decided it was too late unless he ran back to the country, and the prickling of his neck warned him he didn't have the time.

He'd just have to trust that tomorrow night the rogues would pick up the trail in the same place they were forced to abandon it tonight.

He could see the first faint lightening of dawn by the time he reached a rooftop a couple of blocks from Jude's. He paused again, and in that instant, despite the wind, he heard a stealthy movement.

They had posted a sentry near the office. There might be more than one.

He sniffed the air and quickly homed in on the scent's direction. It was upwind of him, not too far away. He could risk waiting it out, for the other would have to find refuge from the light soon. Or he could attack.

He knew which idea he preferred.

He dropped the two coats on the rooftop and began a quick but stealthy movement toward the source of the scent. On high alert, his senses sharpened even more, easily picking out colors and shapes from among shadows.

He smelled blood.

Merde! A newborn? Or simply one of the rogues feeding just before sleep? Either way he had made up his mind. There would be one less vampire when the sun arose.

Not only his speed, which protected him from human eyes, aided him now. Over the centuries he had practiced moving soundlessly, even for a vampire. *Practice makes perfect,* he thought almost wryly as he leaped to the next roof. Even his shoes had been chosen with that in mind.

But a feeding vampire was also less than alert, and that helped him, too. Focused on dining, absorbed in the blood hunger, his quarry would not be as quick to act.

Then he saw the hunched vampire, saw the body it was bent over. Either a rogue leaving a statement or a newborn. The savagery of the attack on the human disgusted him. There was no need for that kind of wallowing in a kill.

Unless you were a newborn and out of control.

Luc's neck prickled again, but this time from awareness of danger. Newborns were stronger. They had to be to survive their creators. Many a vampire had changed his mind about a newborn when faced with the reality of what he or she had just created. Other vampires generally loathed them because they made a mess that could draw attention to the reality of their supposedly mythical existence.

So a newborn *had* to be stronger.

And he was pretty sure that was what he saw on the next roof.

But a newborn, even more than an adult, was less likely to maintain situational awareness despite the blood hunger. Much less likely. They hadn't learned how to control themselves at all.

Making his decision, Luc stopped worrying about stealth and opted for speed.

Not until Luc stood right behind him did the newborn look up from his victim, his face covered with blood.

At the mere sight of another vampire, no questions needed to be asked. The newborn sensed the danger instantly and sprang to his own defense. Luc had faced this before and thought himself prepared.

Nothing, however, could really prepare him for the full-out assault of a newborn.

The other had a serious edge in sheer strength. But Luc had another edge: he was still thinking. While the other responded at an atavistic level, he could be outmaneuvered and jockeyed into a deadly position.

And the sky was lightening even more, probably barely detectible to human eyes, if at all, but to a vampire's eyes it almost looked like flame on the horizon. The newborn would be helplessly aware of that, too, driven by a need to protect himself as well as a need to get to his hole before the sun turned him to ash.

Luc, however, had an idea of just how much longer he actually had, which was longer than the newborn's instincts would be telling him.

He jumped back as the newborn leaped at him, and whipped around the other as he flew through the air. When the newborn passed him, Luc felt the searing pain of fire as the other raked him across the shoulder through his shirt. His own lifeblood, already low, began to run down his arm and chest.

He swore again but didn't pause. A pause could get him killed.

The newborn leaped yet again, and this time Luc moved into him, grabbing his legs and then hurling him halfway across the roof.

The newborn landed like an upended turtle, then sprang to his feet with a snarl.

At that instant the first light of day struck his face. He froze for an instant, shocked by the pain, though he was not yet suffering any damage.

Luc saw the fear in the other's eyes, saw the hesitation, the moment at which the newborn decided it might be better to run to his hole.

He waited a split second and then, just as the newborn turned to flee, Luc sprang.

He caught the newborn in midleap, bringing him down on his face. It was like riding a bucking horse, almost impossible to keep the other pinned.

Luc felt scratches to his thighs as the other clawed at him, but he ignored the wounds. The newborn was thrashing so hard it was almost impossible, but he reached for the head. Hard to hang on to, for the newborn was stronger and twisted wildly to escape the grip. With a massive effort, Luc dug his fingers in, gripping hair and skin, refusing to let go.

The newborn screamed, fighting, but Luc hung on, determined not to let the other escape even as he felt the dawn light burning him, too. He no longer cared if they became a pair of burning torches. He could not let the newborn escape alive.

Then, with one mighty, sharp twist, he snapped the newborn's neck.

He didn't wait. He didn't have time to wait. He vaulted off the body, slid down the side of the building into the shadows as fast as he could and took off for Jude's office.

Chapter 12

"Where is he?" Dani demanded.

Jude had retreated to his inner office but left the door open a crack. "He has time."

"It's dawn."

"He just has to keep to the shadows. There's still time."

But Jude sounded sleepy, and Dani was sure Luc must be feeling the same thing. The clock on the computer in front of her as she sat at Chloe's desk told her that actual sunrise had passed nearly a full minute ago.

Her heart was pounding with anxiety and she could barely hold still. But she had to. Jude had told her how to view the monitor and buzz Luc in when he arrived. Now she couldn't afford to be even two steps away from the button.

It was past dawn.

"What happens?" she finally asked.

Jude's reply was delayed. "Worst case? He falls asleep and when the first rays of the sun hit him he wakes up a torch. That's not going to happen. Luc's been around long enough to know the ropes."

"Dear God," she whispered, unable to bear even imagining it. Her entire chest squeezed as if it were bound in steel bands, and drawing a deep breath became almost impossible.

Just as she thought she was going to shatter from the tension, she heard the buzzer and saw Luc's face in the camera. At once she hit the button to let him in.

She heard his steps in the darkened hallway and forced herself to wait. He was not moving quickly.

When he stepped into the light, she gasped. One side of his face appeared red, as if slightly burned. Blood soaked his shirt and his pants. Panic and horror filled her. Seldom had she felt the pangs of seeing someone she cared about so badly hurt, and it hurt her more deeply than any physical wound.

"I am all right," he said, but he didn't sound all right. He sounded weak and worn.

She leaped up immediately and went to him, slipping an arm around his waist. "What do I need to do?"

"Nothing. I will heal. I need food. Jude?"

"Here." The door to the inner office had opened and Jude stood there, looking sleepy. "Get in here before the sun gets into the office."

Dani didn't know how much she was really helping, but she kept her arm around Luc as he shuffled into Jude's office. He sank into a chair as if he were a falling stone and leaned forward.

She heard Jude behind them, closing and locking his office door. There were no windows in here, but she was quite sure that ultimately that only protected them from death. They would still need to sleep.

"Blood will help you heal faster?" she asked.

"I'll get him some," Jude said.

Before he could do so, Dani pushed up her sleeve and held her wrist right under Luc's mouth. "Drink," she said.

"No," he whispered.

"Oh, shut up," Jude snapped. "You know live blood will work faster and we need you fit at sunset. The lady is offering. A gentleman never refuses a lady."

A near laugh escaped Luc. "Have you never?"

Before Jude could retort, however, Luc sighed, ran his tongue over Dani's arm. She heard Jude go into his bedroom, but sensation utterly distracted her. She couldn't feel the puncture, indeed couldn't feel anything except the sudden wakening of unimaginable pleasure. Never would she have dreamed that feeding a vampire could be nearly as wonderful as making love to one.

His arm reached up after just a couple of seconds and snared her, drawing her onto his lap.

"Forgive me, *ma belle,*" he said hoarsely. Then he nuzzled into her neck, she felt the cool lap of his tongue, and then everything inside her exploded with delight.

She was helpless to stop him, even if she wanted to. Instead, she reached up a hand to cup the back of his head and hold him even closer. She could hear his heart, could feel hers settle into an identical rhythm, a rhythm that soon pulsed through her entire body until even her womanhood throbbed in time with it.

Her head fell back as she gave herself up to sheer enchantment and passion. He had shown her the incredible bliss of a lover's touches, but never had she imagined she could reach the same place when he drank from her.

The moments that passed became as intense as any lovemaking they'd shared. Maybe more intense. Pinwheels of light exploded behind her eyelids, and her body throbbed so hard she knew climax was only moments away.

Her thighs tightened, seeking pressure to answer the need. Her head tipped to one side to grant him better access. With each pull of his mouth, she felt that pull echo in her groin. She had never known anything this erotic. Never imagined it.

All he did was drink, and her core grew heavy and wet. Her breasts felt as if he touched them; her nipples grew so hard they ached. Simply by drinking from her, he wrapped her in shackles of passion so strong they might have been steel.

Her hips rocked helplessly, her body entered the rhythm of his own heart, beating faster and faster as he grew stronger with each mouthful of her blood.

Just a little longer. Just a bit more…

But suddenly he tore his mouth from her. "No more," he said. "I'll take too much."

Still sitting on his lap, feeling dazed by the sudden change, Dani blinked as she looked at him, trying to understand why it had stopped. Why it had needed to stop.

Then the moment was totally interrupted by Jude. "Here, have a bag. I'm sure you didn't get enough from Dani, to judge by the blood on your clothes."

While Dani was still trying to recover her grip on the world around her, Luc took the bag and drained it. Then he licked the last shiny remnants from his mouth and looked at her.

She saw that already the burn was fading from his face.

"I can't stay awake much longer," he said.

"You two take my bedroom," Jude said. "I can stay out here in the office. It's almost as well protected, and I'll be available if anyone shows up."

"My mother should be coming," Dani said. "Besides, what difference does it make who uses which room when you're both going to be dead, anyway?"

A quiet chuckle shook Luc's chest. Even Jude laughed.

"The lady has a point," Luc said. "But if your mother sees what I have done, she will probably kill me the instant I awake."

Dani shook her head. "She won't see. I'll hide it."

"And the coats." Luc paused, his eyelids drooping. "I left your coats on a rooftop several blocks away."

"So what happened to you?" Dani demanded. "You obviously got attacked."

"I did the attacking. A newborn. One less to face come nightfall. But the jackets…I don't know if it's a problem." He seemed to be drifting away.

"You two go to bed," Dani said. "Just give me a general idea where the coats are and I'll have my mother get them. She can have someone bring them here."

Much as she didn't want to, she gave in to the reality and slid off Luc's lap. "Bed," she said. "Both of you. I can keep watch with the help of my pack."

Jude handed her a key card and made her remember six numbers. "That'll get you into my bedroom if you need to wake us for some reason."

"Okay. Go now. Sheesh, the two of you are dead on your feet."

But after she heard the dead bolts thud into place, she stood there feeling very alone and very afraid. She had some idea of Luc's incredible strength. That a newborn could have injured *him* filled her with horror, enough to make her mouth go dry.

She reminded herself that Luc had come back alive and in one piece. Despite this knowledge, she stood swaying for a few moments, trembling a bit as she tried to deal with what had happened and what might have happened.

And dreading what would happen as soon as her pack smelled her.

There was a shower in the front office off Chloe's bedroom. Dani took advantage of it, scrubbing herself thoroughly. She found fresh clothes in the bag she'd packed when she left her apartment. She even used alcohol to wipe the tiny wounds Luc had inflicted before she covered them up. Everything she could do to lessen the odors of Luc and of his having drunk from her.

She stared at the pricks on her wrist and her neck, though, wondering why they weren't yet healing. She was used to having her wounds heal swiftly, and small ones in very short order. These remained, like marks. Something about vampire bites?

She had healed from the attack by those four vampires, but perhaps it had taken longer than usual. How would she know? She had never really had an opportunity to assess her wounds that night. She just hoped these marks vanished entirely before her mother arrived. There was no question in her mind that Lucinda would smell them as long as they remained.

She settled on the couch in the front office to nap

as much as she could while awaiting either a call or a visit from her mother. She honestly hoped it would be a call.

All she knew for certain right now was that she didn't need to fear vampires until sunset. Now all she had to fear was her own family.

That somehow seemed far worse.

Exhausted, she curled up on the couch and tried to absorb what had happened to her when Luc had drunk from her. She throbbed at the mere memory of it and replayed it in her mind. She was beginning to understand why Luc feared making an addict of her.

Because she already wanted that experience again. She was eager for it. The need still pounded in her blood like some heady drug, and permanent withdrawal seemed impossible to bear.

That realization lifted her from the edge of slumber and slammed her with fear. *Addiction.* He had warned her, she hadn't listened, and when he was weakened she had forced him to do what he had so far resisted.

Oh, man, had she lost her mind? Looking at the past few days, she could well believe it. She had given her soul to a vampire, and she wasn't even sure he wanted it.

But even upset couldn't win over exhaustion, and sleep found her quickly, releasing her for just a little while from all the questions, fears and anxieties that had beset her since she was attacked.

* * *

She didn't get much sleep. The barred window above and behind Chloe's desk that let in the light from the street hadn't brightened all that much by the time she heard the door buzzer sound.

Her heart skittered into high gear and she pushed herself up from the couch, hoping against hope that it would be some human who wanted to consult Jude, even though his hours were clearly posted outside.

Rubbing her eyes, she staggered to the desk and looked at the view from the outside security camera. It was Lucinda, bundled almost like an Eskimo.

She pressed the button to talk. "Mom?"

"Yes. Let me in, Dani."

"Just you?"

Lucinda sighed. "Yes. What's going on?"

"I just wondered." Stupid question. Of course it put her mother on alert. But she wanted to know how much she would be facing. She pressed the buzzer, glimpsed the top of Lucinda's hood as she passed the camera then watched the door close.

Lucinda arrived in the office seeming to radiate cold from outside. Her parka was made of old wolf pelts and fur, from wolves who had died of natural causes in the past. No lycan ever killed a wolf if it could be avoided, but when they died their pelts were treasured by those who found them.

She also carried Jude's and Dani's coats. "What

were these doing out there? We found them when we were tracking."

"Luc had to kill a newborn just at dawn. He dropped them and didn't have time to go back for them."

"Ah." Lucinda tossed them on the couch. "And you. What is going on with you?"

"Jude brought me back here while Luc laid the trail."

Lucinda sat in a chair facing Dani across the desk. "And you've been left to guard on your own?"

"What do I have to guard? The vampires are out of action until sunset."

"Which means you and I get to talk without inhibition for the first time since this began."

Dani tensed again. When her mother started talking like that, something unpleasant was about to come up.

"You smell different," Lucinda said.

"I'm hanging out with a different crowd."

"You were hanging out with a different crowd two nights ago. No, you smell *different*. Not like us any longer."

Dani tried to keep her breathing regular, her pulse rate down, but she was sure she didn't succeed. "I haven't changed, Mom. I'm still me."

"But you've done something you shouldn't have." She sniffed several times. "Oh, Dani, I told you not to let him take your blood."

"He was injured! He needed it!"

Lucinda frowned, her eyes saddening. “You can’t become one of them.”

“I won’t.”

“But you’re halfway there. You let a bloodsucker take your blood.”

Dani’s throat tightened. “Luc needed it.”

“His scent not only clings around you now, it’s *in* you. You smell more like one of them now.”

“But I’m not. I’m the same Dani I’ve always been. A lycan who isn’t lycan, a human who isn’t human, a shape-shifter who can’t shape-shift. I am not a vampire.”

“I know. I can tell. But you’re so very close right now.”

“I did what I needed to do. For *me,* Mom. For me.”

“Is that where your path lies now?”

Dani felt her mouth tremble. “I don’t know,” she whispered. Then she added more strongly, “Luc doesn’t want me that way. He’s made that clear. So I just did what I needed to do to help him heal. Is that so wrong?”

Lucinda didn’t answer for long moments. “Perhaps not under the present circumstances. But take care you go no further. Right now it’s going to be hard enough to control the pack if they smell you.”

“Then let them smell me right now. Let’s get this over with.”

Lucinda shook her head. “No. Not now. The smell

may fade by darkfall and we have a serious problem to deal with. I've called in more of the pack."

Dani gripped the edge of the desk, tensing. "What's going on?"

"We tracked those rogues last night. They followed the trail your friend left to the edge of town. It was a good trail, and I think they'll follow it tonight. But I left some of your cousins behind to watch the city. There are more vampires now."

Dani drew a shocked breath. "How many? Newborns?"

"I can't tell a newborn from an adult by scent alone. We counted sixteen. We may be able to get rid of some of them before darkfall."

"Mom, you've got to be careful. Vampires can wake up to defend themselves even from their death sleep."

One corner of Lucinda's mouth lifted. "They can't hide from the sun."

"But they're already hidden."

"We can use mirrors. The sun will be on them before they know we're coming."

For the first time in hours, Dani felt like smiling. "I like that. How many of them can you get to?"

"I'm not sure yet. Some have been much cagier in hiding themselves. Others are barely protected. And we're not absolutely certain there are only sixteen."

Dani nodded. "I'm going with you."

"I told you to wait until the smell in your blood fades."

Dani shook her head. "I have to do this. And the pack is just going to have to get used to it or tear me to shreds." She lifted her chin. "There are some things *I* need to do, Mom. And you need to understand that."

"I understood at least a little when you chose to leave us for life as a normal. It seemed to me you would be happier, and you haven't been happy for a long time. But I'm not sure I can condone this path you've chosen."

"I haven't chosen anything," Dani said hotly. "I was almost killed by bloodsuckers. Other bloodsuckers have saved me and protected me. But I am *damn* sick of being baggage!"

Lucinda was shocked. "Language!"

"I have some more bad human words if you want to hear them. The point is I have as much stake in this as anyone, and I'm not going to be shoved into a corner because you, the pack or the vampires think I'm useless and weak."

Lucinda's frown deepened. "You know how some of your cousins are."

"They need to grow up. We're facing a threat and it's not just a threat to vampires and humans. You don't want to live in a world where vampires run everything. You couldn't move far enough away to find peace. We made an alliance, and whether they like how I smell is irrelevant. They'll just have to live with it."

"Some things are instinctual."

"And others are learned. Judging by the way I've changed my thinking, it's my opinion that this response is learned. It's also my opinion that things have changed. Until the last few days, when was the last time any lycan actually talked to a vampire? I know what Luc said about us."

"And that was?"

"That he had absolutely no interest in us unless we threatened him. Neither Jude nor Creed seemed in the least disturbed that I'm lycan. The only one who was disturbed was the human who works for Jude, Chloe, and she got over it fast. So maybe it's time to make peace."

Lucinda lowered her head, clearly thinking. Finally she sighed. "I don't know. Things are different now from the past, I'll agree. In the past we objected to the bloodsuckers taking unwilling mortals, and when they did, we sometimes intervened. You know we have our own idea about what is fair prey, and humans are not. We may share different shapes, but we share the same hearts and minds as humans."

"Yes."

"Maybe the bloodsuckers have evolved."

"Then maybe we should, as well."

Lucinda gave her a piercing look, as if she could read Dani's heart and mind. "All this talk of peace will give the pack indigestion. Let's just start with dealing with our common threat."

"And letting me help."

"Before you help, I'm going to bring you a new

wolfskin jacket. That parka of yours smells entirely too much like a certain bloodsucker. We need to get through the first half minute without you being killed. Time enough for reason to reassert."

"All right. But where can you get me a jacket?"

"I brought an extra. In fact it's yours, the one you left behind." Lucinda smiled wistfully. "I guess part of me hoped you'd come home with us. I see that is not to be. I'll be back as soon as I can."

"And I'm going to help, right?"

"Yes, daughter, you're going to help. I just hope your father doesn't blow a gasket."

Dani didn't bother to argue that she was an adult now. In the pack, being an adult meant accepting your place in the hierarchy and obeying orders. Defying her mother was defying that order. It put her squarely outside the pack in more ways than just her odor.

Once again she felt that grief that she would never, ever be a true member of her pack. But it was an old grief, a bittersweet one in a way, one she had fully accepted when she'd made her decision to move away and live life as a normal.

Life as a normal? She didn't know whether to laugh or cry at that thought. Certainly she'd been normal for only a few months. Look at her now: fallen in with a bunch of bloodsuckers, making her own mother upset at every turn, possibly facing the hostility of the pack she loved as much as life itself.

That was *normal?*

* * *

Lucinda returned around noon. The storm had given way to a day of nearly painful brilliance as the sun glittered off every bit of snow from a cloudless, piercingly blue sky.

Wrapped in the wolfskin coat she had once abandoned, mukluks on her feet, Dani left a note behind and went outside with her mother. Jude had given her the key card and pass code for his inner sanctum, but she doubted he used the same ones for his front door. Regardless, she tucked the card in an inside pocket for safety.

Outside, she blinked in the nearly blinding light of a winter day.

"We need to get over the first hump," Lucinda said.

"Me?"

"Yes. We can't roam the streets in wolf form because we'll attract too much notice, but they're going to meet you in that form at an out-of-the-way place. I've explained, but I can't promise they aren't agitated."

Dani swallowed hard and nodded. Her mother was right to be worried. There was a level at which the pack acted to protect itself that not even an alpha could prevent. Survival trumped everything, and if the pack took this as survival, she'd be dead soon.

Oddly enough, thinking about her possible death dragged her thoughts straight to Luc. He'd been right to fear a claiming, she admitted. Nobody could be sure that something wouldn't happen to rupture it. If even a portion of what he'd intimated about his suffering over Natasha was true, she hoped he'd escaped it with her. She never wanted him to long for death because the pain was too great to bear.

But even thinking of him was not enough to stop her. For once in her life, she had to do something in concert with her pack. To be truly useful to them in some way. The inability to do that had driven her away. Now, though she might never go back, she would at least know she was strong enough, sure enough, useful enough to work with them against a threat.

Lucinda drove them in a huge black SUV. "I thought we didn't own cars," Dani remarked.

"We don't. We judged one might be necessary this time and we can afford it. It's been very useful, actually."

Of course her pack could afford it. That had never been the question. Because they were shape-shifters, they couldn't live entirely without money; they had human needs to meet, as well. A number of the pack had found human jobs to bring home money and worked them as long as they could.

"Is Derek still running our investments?"

"Who else would have the patience?"

Dani might have giggled if uneasiness hadn't been growing with each block they drove. Luc would be appalled by what she was doing, and come to think of it, so was she. Had she become so stubborn about proving something that it had led her to folly? And what was it that she was trying to prove again? That she could get along on her own? That she didn't need the pack's protection? Or was this all about a hurt little girl who simply had never been able to do what everyone around her could do?

But her inner demons kept pushing her on into more and more precarious situations. Being helpful to the pack, being helpful to the vampires, being helpful to humans…it didn't matter anymore which she did, she just *had* to do something.

Unfortunately, that was probably the most dangerous state of mind to be in.

"Don't get out of the car until I tell you," Lucinda warned as they pulled into a deserted alley. Trash was blowing around over the fresh snowfall that appeared utterly undisturbed. The enclosing buildings showed blank facades of brick, and the few windows there once had been were filled in with more bricks.

One of the unfortunate parts of town, she thought.

Not the kind of place her pack usually liked to be. There was an open end down the way, but the pack was nearly claustrophobic except inside their own dens and dwellings. With good reason.

Lucinda put the car in Park and tooted the horn once, briefly.

The gathering began, one and two at a time. Apparently they had been nearby. They came from both ends of the alley, leaving paw prints, stirring up the snow. Soon there were a dozen swirling around the car.

Dani might have smiled at the sight of them if she hadn't been so nervous. She had seen the pack hunt and kill, and as a normal she wouldn't stand a chance. Their restless rovings, however, were so familiar that the sight warmed her, anyway. In wolf form they seldom held still. The urge to keep moving was powerful, only occasionally giving way as they got older to the need for something like sitting by a warm fire. And that was something they usually did in human form.

Lucinda climbed out, gave a whistle and led the pack away from the car. Dani watched, wishing she could hear her mother, but for now she obeyed as she was always supposed to obey and all too often hadn't. The alpha had told her to stay. No matter how anxious she grew, no matter how much she just wanted to get this over with, this was one time she must behave.

Finally Lucinda came back to the car, opened the door and leaned in. "They've found some more. Worse, your father thinks that the most we can burn today will be four or five. That means we may well meet a dozen or more of your bloodsucker friends…."

"They're not my friends. They're rogues." Unfortunately, that slip of her mother's tongue told her a lot and made her heart sink.

"The rogues," Lucinda corrected herself. "We're

going to have our hands full tonight. But at least we can cut their numbers. Are you ready?"

Dani didn't answer. She simply opened the car door and walked toward the waiting pack.

As she got closer, fangs were bared, and growls emanated from deep, huge chests. She kept walking, anyway. This was her family. If they couldn't accept her any longer, then they would do what they had to. Her heart hammered nervously, as she expected death to strike at any moment.

But with each step, she noted a change. First one and then another of her cousins stopped growling. Fangs disappeared. Heads cocked questioningly.

Smell or not, they were facing her change in odor. Dealing with it.

At last she stood only a foot away. For an eternity nothing seemed to move, then the pack swirled around her, smelling her, nudging her with their noses. She took the buffeting, recognizing it for what it was. They intended her no harm. They were simply absorbing her difference.

Finally, the youngest of them, her brother Max, stood on his hind legs, rested his forepaws on her shoulders and looked into her eyes. The pack seemed to freeze and hold its breath.

"Hi, Max," she said. Ordinarily she would have dug her fingers into his ruff and given him a good scratch. She didn't dare do that yet.

He held her gaze, his own blue eyes piercing. Then he gave her a sloppy lick on her cheek. With that, the decision was made. The pack surrounded her again, this time with high tails and grins. Thrilled at her reception, she scratched every neck she could reach.

"All right," Lucinda said, her tone conveying more relief than she probably realized. "We've got work to do."

But of course it was not over. At that moment Jerrod came loping up the alley, transforming over his last few strides until he towered over her, fur clad but human.

"What have you done?" he asked. For once he didn't thunder. The question sounded almost sorrowful.

"What I had to, Dad," she said with as much firmness as she could muster.

"I may kill that bloodsucker."

"Don't you dare lay a hand on him. I've always disappointed you, so why should you care now?"

The pack froze. Back talking the alpha male was dangerous.

"Disappointed me? When have I ever said that?"

"You never had to say it. Now we have to live with what is. I am not fully pack. I am not fully human. But neither am I vampire. You're just going to have to learn to live with it, Dad. I can't be something I'm not. I have to find my own way."

Tension crackled on the air. Max was the one who broke it, edging in between the two of them and nudging each of them with his nose.

Finally Jerrod reached out and embraced his daughter. "Just don't become one of *them.*"

He didn't wait for her answer before he melted back into wolf form.

"All right," Lucinda said firmly, "we have no time to waste. Dani and I will transport the mirrors to our first target. We'll see you there."

The pack took off again while Dani and Lucinda climbed back into the car. It was a moment before Lucinda turned over the ignition.

"Whew," she said.

Dani looked at her. "It went well."

"Your father was the one I was worried about. He's so damn hardheaded. I was fairly certain the others would come around as long as Jerrod didn't become stupid with rage. And you know Max adores you. You practically raised him for me."

Along with quite a few other pups who still weren't full grown. Dani missed them desperately and hoped that as soon as this was over she would be allowed to go home and see them. At this point, though, she wasn't sure their acceptance of her would last past the immediate crisis. She could only hope.

"Why did you elect to use mirrors?" she asked. "I know if the entire pack attacked them one at a time, they wouldn't stand a chance."

"We don't want any avoidable injuries, but most important, we don't want them to guess we're involved. It would ruin tonight's surprise."

By the light of a flashlight and the pack's excellent noses, they found the first vampire in a basement without windows, at the back of a long corridor. He slept against a wall, behind a closed door, looking like a derelict. Only his smell gave him away.

The pack transformed. A chain of mirrors was set up down the hallway with one reflecting light right into the room. Before they focused the beam, Dani told them to wait.

Figuring the vampire wouldn't recognize her as a threat, she gathered her courage and stole into the basement room to pull away the rags that kept him half-buried, as if he wanted to look like part of a trash heap. With every step, she remembered all too vividly how a vampire could overpower her and rip into her. Her mouth turned as dry as dust, and each step was an internal battle. To her relief, he didn't even stir.

Then she stepped back into the hallway. It took the pack less than ten seconds to focus an intense beam of sunlight on the sleeping vampire.

He woke at once, screaming, and tried to dodge the light. Jerrod, who held the mirror nearest the door, shifted enough to keep him in its beam.

It happened so fast it was hard to believe. One second he was screaming, the next he was flaming. And then he was ash. It horrified Dani.

"Wow," she whispered, closing her eyes. She couldn't bear the thought of that happening to Luc.

Yet it might have this very morning as he fought that newborn. Hadn't he come back looking a bit singed?

She turned quickly away and headed past her pack back to the car. She needed to stop seeing Luc in this, she thought as she squared her shoulders. No weakening now. She had demanded to be part of this.

But now she had to cope with it.

Chapter 13

"You killed how many?" Luc asked. He had just emerged from the inner sanctum and received the news from Dani and her mother. Jude followed on his heels.

"Four," Dani said.

"It's all we had time for," Lucinda said regretfully. "The sun got too low and the mirrors wouldn't send a strong enough beam, as we discovered with the fifth. But there are still approximately a dozen left."

"And perhaps some newborns who'll awake tonight," Luc said. He looked at Dani. "And you helped with this?"

"She most certainly did," Lucinda said a bit sharply. "My daughter has become quite stubborn. I don't suppose you can talk her out of going along tonight. I can't imagine what earthly use she can be when vampires and lycans face vampires."

Dani's cheeks grew hot with anger. "Why not just say it, Mom? I'm useless because I can't shift."

"Dani..."

"No, I don't want to hear it. You can all pretend it doesn't matter, but I know it does. I've known it since I failed to shift."

Lucinda sighed. "I just worry about you. You're my *daughter*."

But Luc's eyes had crinkled at the corners and he smiled at Dani. "Feel better, my Valkyrie?"

"Much. And I'm not staying home tonight." She turned to her mother. "You said it yourself. If blood lust overcomes the pack once the fight begins, they might not distinguish between vampires, but they'll distinguish me. I might be the only control you have."

Lucinda frowned, but didn't deny it. "You can't keep up with us."

Another reminder. Boy, those reminders were being poured all over her today. But this time she didn't cringe. She just gave her mother a steady stare. Just as she was about to mention that she could drive, Luc spoke.

"It will be my honor to carry her. She won't slow me down."

Lucinda rounded on him. "What kind of being do you claim to be, fighting to protect yourself and humans, but unwilling to protect my daughter?"

"I would give my life to protect your daughter, Madam Wolf, but I will not wound her by suggesting she is useless. She is not and never has been useless. Despite her severe injuries, she managed to fight off four vampires before they killed her. How do you think it is that I found her alive? Because she fought. And why is it that one of them came back to kill her later? Because they never intended to leave her alive, they simply waited until they felt she would be weakened by her injuries."

Lucinda continued to glare at him.

"Did you not see her courage today?" Luc asked quietly.

After several beats, Lucinda sighed. "She has great courage."

"Indeed. So unless you wish this to turn into a fight right here and now, I will carry Dani with me into the battle."

"You will protect her?"

"Haven't I said so? In the end, however, it may be Dani who protects me…or someone else."

Lucinda turned back to Dani, her eyes dimmed and troubled. "I never wanted you to feel this way about yourself, Dani. Never. We love you. But you have stepped out of the hierarchy."

Dani swallowed hard as her throat tightened. She had just been told that in the most important way possible she was no longer part of the pack. They might still love her, but she no longer had a place. She blinked hard, keeping back the tears.

Luc surprised her. He slipped swiftly to her side and put his arm around her. "Damn your hierarchy," he said, his voice tight with anger. "No wonder she felt compelled to leave you."

"Luc, please," Dani said, her voice thickened by the tightness in her throat. "This has to wait. Everything has to wait except the rogues. They must be out there moving even now." She looked at her mother from eyes as hot as coals. "They're being followed?"

Lucinda nodded, her expression stony.

"Then let's get on with the plan. Now."

Lucinda hesitated only a moment before heading out the door.

"My goodness," Jude drawled. "Dani just gave an order to her alpha. And the alpha obeyed."

A tear escaped Dani's eye and she managed a weak laugh. "I guess I did."

Luc wiped the tear tenderly away with a forefinger. "Bundle up, little wolf. It's time."

He wasn't too thrilled with her wolfskin coat and mukluks, though. He wrinkled his nose. "Must you?"

"They're what I have. Get used to it."

He sighed. "So very difficult. You are becoming quite the alpha yourself." But then he winked, taking the sting out of the words.

The night was clear and cold, with a breeze blowing toward the southeast. "That'll make it easier to track them," Luc remarked to Jude.

"Much, for the lycans at least."

The vampires had decided to backtrack the path Luc had laid last night while the lycans would follow the vamps out of town, thus bringing them at the rogues from opposing directions.

Dani, clinging to Luc's back, asked, "Will they still be able to smell the track? It's been hours since you left it and we've had four more inches of snow."

"They can," Luc assured her. "In one way we are like your pack. Our sense of smell."

"They're not my pack anymore."

"Don't lose hope, Dani. There will be time to work this all out later."

If they survived.

With Luc carrying her, Dani had too much time to think. She couldn't see the sights whizzing by and could barely tell the difference when he leaped or when he ran, it all happened so fast.

The pain of what her mother had said remained like a knife in her heart. Even knowing it was true, knowing she had chosen a path away from her pack, it hurt to hear it stated so baldly.

Being broken, as Luc had called her, was a fact she hadn't been able to ignore or escape. So she had come to this place to live as a normal, even though she would never exactly be one of them, either, not given what she knew and how she had been raised.

She hadn't even allowed herself to date, though she had been asked out a couple of times, because her lycan heritage loomed over everything. How could she explain it to a human? Would he even accept it? And what if she said nothing, married and had a fully lycan child?

Even as she had struck out to make a new life, she had been trapped in the cage of what she was. Still.

Until Luc. It really didn't seem to trouble him that she was a broken wolf, part lycan, part human. He knew enough that she hadn't had to offer any awkward explanations, and he'd known it from the start.

Yet still he had made love to her. Held her close. Drunk of her. It would probably never be more than that, but it had given her a taste of being truly accepted, a sense of belonging, however brief.

That might all end tonight. She might be left with something very much like the longing and anguish Luc had said he had felt over the loss of Natasha. It might even stop her from ever making another connection for fear of being left alone and lonely again.

But as she pressed her face to Luc's back, she knew one thing for certain: she wouldn't have missed this experience for the world, even if she didn't survive the night.

She realized they were out of the city only because the world grew brighter. The blur became mostly white and the smells changed from the crowded odors of cars and people to the fresh odor of a world wearing snow. Overhead the moon still seemed almost full when she could manage to focus on it long enough.

But mostly she kept her face buried against Luc.

He was moving so fast that the wind cut almost like a knife, as if she were riding a rocket-propelled sled.

When they halted, they were far out into the country, pausing along a line of trees that edged an open field. Luc set her down in snow that nearly reached her knees.

"Okay," he said. "Do you want me to call Lucinda or do you want to do it?"

"I'll do it," Dani said. No way was she going to let her mother's harsh statement cow her. She was independent now, that had been made perfectly clear. No longer part of the hierarchy also meant something else: she was no longer pack but she could now claim equality. A lone wolf, maybe, but bowing to no alpha.

Lucinda answered swiftly. "They're turning off the road, eleven of them together. We suspect some may have remained in town, but these eleven are following the trail. The wind still favors us."

Then, without another word, Lucinda disconnected. Words unspoken seemed to tear Dani's heart. No *I love you*. No wish for good luck. Nothing.

She drew a steadying breath and passed the report along.

"It won't be long now," Jude remarked. "We need to choose our spot quickly."

Luc swung her up again, the world blurred, then she found herself in a copse of trees.

"This looks good enough," Luc said. "I only hope

the wind continues to favor us or they'll smell the freshening of our scent."

"Not until they get here," Jude said. "Not with the wind blowing our scent away."

For the first time Dani realized that the wind had picked up. Within the copse it came in gusts, but just beyond the trees she could see snow devils whirling and dancing across open fields.

"I'm going to put you in a tree," Luc said to her. "We need to keep this fight on the ground so your pack can help, but I need for you to stay high so your scent drifts away faster."

"What do you want me to do except hide?"

He cupped both her cheeks with chilly hands. "Do what you must. You will know. From here on, we wait. When they arrive, we fight." He kissed her hard, as if he wanted to drink the very soul from her body, and left her feeling a bit light-headed. "I trust you to know how you can help and when. I also trust you to know when you'll only hinder us."

That was, she realized, more trust than she'd ever been given. The choices had been left utterly in her hands.

Jude cocked his head. "I think I hear their approach. Quickly, get her up there."

The next thing she knew, she was sitting in a tree about ten feet above ground, in a V created by limb and trunk. Up there she really felt the wind and understood why they wanted her there. Her scent was being blown away to the east, away from the approaching vampires.

Yet she had a clear view of everything from up here. She watched as Jude and Luc stepped to the edge of the copse and waited, as if they were alone. Creating the impression that the trail the rogues followed had been the right one.

But there were just the two of them against eleven who approached. Dani wondered how far behind the pack was, but didn't dare make a call. Pulling out her phone, she checked for messages and there was a text:

We have them in sight.

Dani replied just as briefly. *We're ready.* Then she turned off the phone so it could make no revealing sound.

After charging headlong into whatever would happen, time suddenly seemed to grind to a halt. The two vampires stood just within the shadows of the trees, but she doubted they would be concealed for long from the approaching rogues.

They seemed to be carved from stone. She, on the other hand, could barely hold still. Her heart was pounding, surely audible to any vampire paying attention, she started to itch in awkward places considering she was in a tree and her mouth felt as dry as sand. Great timing.

While part of her absolutely hated this waiting, another part of her hoped the moment of conflict never came. A strange wish, considering that it clearly couldn't be avoided, but she was experiencing a definite desire to be elsewhere and elsewhen. She closed her eyes for a moment, imagining that she and Luc lay together somewhere alone, wrapped in each other's arms....

She jerked back to the present when a branch above her trembled enough to plop snow on her head. Luc and Jude still stood like statues, but to her it seemed they had grown somehow stiffer. The rogues must be near.

She sniffed the air and detected the faint odor of strange vampires. It was faint because she didn't fully have her pack's sense of smell—how could she when she was missing a few million scent receptors?—but it was better than human as she had long since discovered.

And now it told her danger was very near.

Oddly enough, as soon as she realized the moment was almost at hand, her heart slowed and steadied, and a calm came over her, leaving her feeling as clearheaded as she ever had in her life. Lycan nature arising? How could she know?

But something in her was itching and ready for this fight now that it had nearly arrived. It was certainly a feeling she'd never had before, perhaps because she'd never been able to run with her pack.

She held her breath, listening, but all she could hear was the wind. Jude and Luc shifted just a tiny bit, as if readying themselves.

And then she heard a sound that would always

thrill her to her soul: a wolf's full-throated howl. Her cousin Alis was near, which meant the pack was ready to circle in and Alis's call was the locator.

But it was only the one howl, one signal, giving away no information as to how many lycans roamed the night.

Still, it might reveal something to the rogues. There were no wolves in this area, and if they were familiar with wolf calls as opposed to the howling of a dog, they might realize what was closing in on them.

Dani hoped they couldn't distinguish. A lone dog that might have been disturbed by their passing wouldn't trouble them. Apparently that's what Lucinda was hoping when she had given Alis her orders.

The howl trailed away quickly, lasting just long enough for the rest of the pack to get the message: the rogues were near and Alis was on their heels.

At last the rogues drew close enough that even Dani could hear them swishing through the deep snow, a murmur like the wind in leaves because they moved so fast and lightly.

Jude and Luc separated, making sure they were two distinct targets and could not be attacked as one. Divide and conquer.

Glancing around, Dani saw a heavy broken branch resting just above her: thick, not too long, but of a size to use as a club or short spear. And the end was sharp. Clinging to the tree trunk, she reached for it and tested it. Despite the frigid temperatures, it was still pliable enough that it shouldn't snap.

Good. She held it close and waited.

That was the point at which she had to admit her own disadvantage, like it or not. What happened next happened so fast she couldn't see it.

Jude and Luc were no longer visible to her as they merged with swiftly moving shadows. Everything blurred because of the vampires' speed.

Her calm gave way to trepidation as she realized why everyone had wanted to keep her out of this. She looked at the stick in her hand and knew it would be useless against beings who moved so fast. She couldn't stand not being able to do anything, but she couldn't see enough to be able to act.

Then a chorus of wolf howls rose, each voice pitched in perfect harmony to the others so that a few wolves could sound like so many more. She had no idea exactly how many of the pack had come for this fight, but from the swelling chorus of howls she knew it had to be eight or nine. And they sounded like twenty. They surrounded her.

A shiver of pure pleasure ran down her spine in response. She would never be immune to her family's calls.

But the rising chorus of howls had an unexpected effect on the two large black shadows just beyond the trees. They froze, instantly dissolving into separate shapes. Eleven vampires plus Jude and Luc.

It seemed to be a moment of indecision on the

part of the rogues. The pack howled again, the chorus rising from a single voice to many, haunting the night. Closer now, much closer.

Jude and Luc both leaped at the vampires frozen in front of them, but they were outnumbered. Something had happened, though. Awareness that wolves were closing in on them had made the rogues edgy, uncertain. They moved slower and as the battle resumed, Dani could make out individual shapes, although not clearly.

Distracted, unsure if the howls threatened them, unsure of whether these were stray wolves or dreaded lycans, the rogues had lost their edge.

Seeing it, Dani slid down out of the tree. They might move too fast for her to fight well, but she was going to Luc and Jude's aid, anyway, especially with her pack so close now. Never having shifted, she had only a vague notion of how well her family would be able to pick out the rogues from the two who were fighting them, especially if they started moving faster. Lycans could see vampires when humans couldn't because they were moving too fast, but what was too fast for lycan eyes?

She knew of only one thing to do: insert herself. It would slow everything down. And even in the blurs before her she recognized Luc.

A howl of a different kind rent the night. A vampire fell to the snow and didn't move. One down, and it was neither Jude nor Luc.

She had barely taken one step forward when she felt a nudge. Looking around she saw Max.

"Can you tell which one is which?" she asked him.

His canine head bobbed a clear yes.

"Then let's go. You'll have to help me."

Max responded with a quick wag of his tail and hurried beside her to the battling clouds. And really, that's what they almost looked like to her, two black clouds from which emerged identifiable shapes from time to time.

"Luc," she said to Max, hoping he would know which one she meant. Well, duh, she thought as Max led the way: he knew which vampire's smell was all over her.

Her appearance with a large wolf beside her caused an almost freeze-frame response. Luc was undisturbed and seized the opportunity to grab a rogue by his head.

In the meantime, Max leaped, grabbing another vampire's arm in his powerful jaws and dragging him down, holding him. Ignoring the enraged shriek, which was nearly deafening, Dani followed Max with her stick.

It was rather late to wonder if driving a stake into a vampire's heart was myth or true, and the possibility of aiming was pretty much out of her control as the vampire whipped about, blurring before her very eyes. But then Alis jumped in and grabbed the rogue's other arm. He still writhed, and from the corner of her eye she saw another vampire coming swiftly to his aid.

She swung around immediately, putting every bit of her body's weight behind the stick as she bashed the second rogue on the side of his head.

"Good job," Luc said, grabbing the stunned vampire and wrenching his head nearly off his neck.

Dani turned back to the one Alis and Max were holding in their powerful grip. He was pushing himself across the snow, trying to get away, but the two lycans dug in their paws and resisted.

Well, if a blow to the head had helped with one... Dani swung. At the instant her stick struck the downed vampire she felt something grab her by her coat and lift her off her feet.

Then she was looking into the dark eyes of a stranger, a rogue. He snarled at her and bared his fangs.

Here we go again, she thought. She still had hold of the stick, but all she could do with it was batter it against his side. He didn't even seem to notice.

Then she heard Luc growl, "Leave my lady alone!"

She never saw what happened next. All of a sudden she was free, and another broken vampire lay in the snow.

"Through the neck," Luc said, pointing at her stick, "or in the eye." Then he returned to the battle.

The vampire held down by Max and Alis was

struggling more sluggishly as dark blood seeped from his arms onto the snow.

"Neck," Dani said sharply.

Max reared up on his hind paws, released the arm he had been biting and went for the rogue's neck. He yelped as the vampire managed to get in a blow, but he didn't stop.

Another one down as Max's jaws clamped on vital tissue.

Dani turned, looking for another target, but found herself blocked by her mother.

Lucinda used her body to push Dani away, and as much as Dani wanted to join the fray, she realized it was pointless. Nine lycans and two vampires seemed to be dealing just fine now with fewer than six rogues.

Two of the wolves would bring a vampire down and hold him or her until someone finished the job. Sometimes it was Luc or Jude, sometimes it was another lycan. And then it was over. Impossibly, silence fell except for the huffing of the wolves. Jude and Luc sported wounds to their faces but they didn't look serious.

Dani looked around. "Max? Max, where are you?"

Her brother trotted over and Dani dropped to her knees in the snow, grabbing him by his ruff. "Are you okay? I heard you yelp."

There was no mistaking the grin he gave her.

"Thank goodness," she said and wrapped her arms around his neck, hugging him.

The last time, she thought. This would probably be the last time she buried her face in his fur. He rested his massive head on her shoulder, hugging her back. But it was not over. She felt the tension in him suddenly and pulled back. A message had been communicated among the pack and she'd been too busy hugging Max to catch the body language of tails.

Sensing that something was about to go very wrong, she rose to her feet.

Jerrod. Her father. He had half shifted back to human form and he was moving toward Luc. "You took my daughter."

Luc stood fast. "I think she makes her own decisions."

"No, you damn vampires put people under a spell. That's what you did to her. My daughter wouldn't consort with your kind, wouldn't let you drink from her willingly."

"Beg to differ," Jude drawled. "Dani can't be vamped. Tried it, you know."

Jerrod whirled on him. Dani ran across trampled snow, leaping over bodies to insert herself between her father, Luc and Jude.

"I did try it," Luc admitted. "But only to find out who she was."

"Didn't work," Jude said lazily. "I saw it myself."

"It's true," Dani said. "They can't control me."

"How would you know?" Jerrod roared. "You'd be the *last* to know."

Suddenly Lucinda was there, also half-transformed. She touched Jerrod's arm but he shoved her hand away. At that the pack started growling menacingly, and Dani honestly couldn't tell whether they blamed the vampires for this extraordinary behavior from Jerrod, or him.

"Dad, I've made every decision myself. By myself."

He opened his mouth and drew a huge breath, apparently ready to start in again, but this time Lucinda would not be denied.

"Jerrod," she said sharply, "remember yourself! You defy my authority in front of the pack and you know what that could mean."

Jerrod clenched and unclenched his fists, clearly seething. He looked at Lucinda. "You would let our daughter go with these bloodsuckers?"

"Each member of the pack makes his or her own decision about whether to remain with the pack or go to another. You know that. We don't have the right to approve or disapprove. Dani has made her choice."

Dani has made her choice? Dani heard those words like stones dropping into her heart. She supposed she *had* made a choice of some kind, mainly in defying her mother about getting involved, but the bottom line was that the choice had been made for her, by faulty genetics and by her mother's own words. She didn't want to give up the pack; she just didn't fit in. Apparently her mother didn't see it that way.

But she hadn't chosen a different pack. Not really. What had happened between her and Luc would probably evaporate quickly once this mess was over. And it was mostly over now. But he had made it so clear that he didn't want to risk claiming her, and that most likely meant that whatever lay between them was short-term only.

The thought nearly broke her heart, but she didn't have time for that now. The tension between the alphas had the pack pacing nervously, not a good thing, and she wasn't surprised when one of them, Carty, snapped at Luc's hand. Just a snap, but expressive nonetheless.

Luc didn't move a muscle. He didn't react at all. Dani, however, was not going to let that pass. She hurried to stand beside him and grabbed Carty's ear.

"No," she said sharply. "They aren't responsible for any of this."

Carty's tail went down and he slunk over to the others.

Lucinda looked at her daughter. "You would have made a great alpha."

"I never had that opportunity. And I really don't want to choose sides, because the way I see it, there are no sides to choose. You are my family. These are my friends."

"Yet you choose to go with them," Jerrod growled.

"They befriended me. They saved me. Now we've made common cause against these rogues. But it was my mother who told me I was out of the hierarchy."

Jerrod whirled toward Lucinda. "You told her that?"

"She refused to obey me. It is our way."

"So," Dani said, through a tightening throat, "I make my way alone now. That is your way."

At that, some of the youngsters came over to her, whining, nudging at her legs, telling her they wanted her to rejoin them. But she couldn't. She would fit with them even less now. Whatever her path, it couldn't include returning north with her pack.

Not her pack. Not anymore. She had to blink so as not to cry.

"I think," Luc said, his voice tight, "that there would be better times to get into this matter. Times with less pressure. We still have a city to finish cleaning out and time is short. Will you join us, Madam Wolf?"

Lucinda hesitated. While awaiting her decision, her mate melted back into wolf form and went to stand with the rest of the pack.

"No," she said. "Not unless Dani calls and says she needs us."

Dani looked at Luc. "Do you think you can handle the rest of them?"

"I doubt there are many more, thanks to Terri's work at the morgue. If newborns appear here and there, the two of us can take care of them." Clearly he wanted nothing more to do with wolves.

Dani swallowed hard and looked at her mother. "Will I see you again?"

Lucinda nodded. "We still love you, even if you choose a path away from us. You know where we are."

Then she shifted and turned, leading the silent pack away.

Before they had gone very far, however, Alis and Max came bounding back to swirl around Dani and whine sadly. She ruffled their fur lovingly then said, "Go before Lucinda gets mad." Her eyes were still on them as they vanished into the night.

Jude looked around at the bodies. "I suppose the sun will take care of them."

Luc agreed. "Burying them won't conceal them from other vampires, and building a pyre would draw quite a bit of attention."

"I should think so," said Jude. "Back to the city, then. There's still work to be done."

Luc reached out and lifted Dani, this time carrying her in her arms. Not by a word or sound did he indicate that he knew she wept silently all the way back.

Chapter 14

A surprise awaited them when they returned to Jude's office. In a shadow, beyond reach of the moon, stood another vampire. Dani stiffened as soon as the smell reached her nose. So did Luc.

"Put me down," she whispered. "You might need to defend yourself."

He lowered her feet to snowy pavement, but kept his arm around her shoulders.

Then Jude said, "Damien! Good heavens, man, where did you come from?"

"I got your message, but I was in Cologne. Do you have any idea how devilishly difficult it has become to cross the Atlantic? The damn customs people are even opening coffins these days because their dogs alert. Now, I ask you, do I smell like an illegal drug or explosive?"

Jude sniffed then laughed. "Not in the least."

Damien moved out of the shadows, showing himself to be about just a couple of inches shorter than six feet. He had raven-black hair, a Teutonic nose and somehow reminded Dani of pictures she had seen of knights engraved on old tombs in European churches.

"I suspect," Damien said, "that I'm too late. I wandered around the city a bit before I came here, but you don't seem to be overwhelmed by other vampires."

"We took out a number of them tonight. At this point we hope we're only dealing with a small handful of newborns and one or two adults."

"Any newborn is a handful," Damien remarked. "More than one is a catastrophe."

Jude let them all into his office and turned on a dim light in deference to Dani.

"It's good to see you again, Damien," Luc remarked. "How is Cologne?"

"As beautiful as ever, though getting a bit too big for my taste. I did get to enjoy the Cathedral bells a few nights ago." He looked at Dani. "Have you ever been there? Well, they ring the bells only on very important occasions these days, maybe four to six times a year. But when they chime… Heavens! First the Dom bells begin…that's the cathedral…a very deep bell at first. And over the next ten minutes or so, other bells chime in and then other churches until the sound is coming from everywhere. It's quite magical."

"It sounds like it." She smiled politely, wondering how Damien fit in, whether he might potentially be a threat and how he would react to her. She was relieved when Luc sat beside her on the couch.

"You must take her there," Damien said to Luc.

Dani caught her breath in astonishment. What did Damien know and how did he know it?

"I'll think about it," Luc agreed. "I've been yearning to get back home, but if travel is as difficult as you say…" He shrugged.

"You can always travel in the wheel well of a plane." Damien chuckled. "It avoids the entire customs problem."

"That's how I crossed last time."

"I wish you had told me. I'd have been here sooner and wouldn't have missed all the fun. I was sorry to hear about Natasha."

Dani looked quickly at Luc, fearing the reminder would cast him down or make him uncomfortable. But he didn't seem to react at all.

"She made some unwise choices" was all Luc said.

Before Damien could pursue the subject, Jude swiftly turned the conversation back to the rogues. "We still have to clean out the city. If you want to help, then we should get right to it. I don't expect we'll finish tonight, but the longer we wait, the more humans will die or be changed."

This time Dani didn't even suggest she accompany them. From what Luc had told her of newborns, she'd be worse than useless; she would be a hindrance since she was exhausted. Without complaint, she accepted Jude's offer to use his bed behind a locked door. She barely had energy left to wash up and change into a nightdress before she dove under the warm covers. She wiggled her toes in pleasure, tried not to think about Lucinda's harsh words and her father's anger, and fell into a sleep so deep she was hardly aware of it when Luc slipped in beside her and wrapped her in his arms.

"Je t'aime. J'ai un amour fou pour toi."

The husky murmur drew her out of sleep and she found herself looking into the inky eyes of night. Luc's head was on the pillow beside hers and he looked straight into her drowsy eyes.

"Huh?" she managed groggily, astonished to be waking to find him alert. She seemed to remember him crawling into bed a while ago. Had the entire day passed already?

The question snapped her awake.

"I said, *'Je t'aime, j'ai un amour fou pour toi.'*"

"I don't understand."

He smiled. "*Je sais.* I know. But when you have grown up speaking a certain language, some things seem to have more meaning in your mother tongue."

"Okay. But you still haven't explained."

"*Ma belle dame,* my little wolf, I said I love you. I said I am crazy with love for you."

Her heart slammed into high gear so fast that she suddenly couldn't breathe. "Crazy?" she repeated, her voice cracking.

"Crazy."

She tried to restrain a wild surge of emotion, tried to retain some sense in a brain that just wanted to melt. "Is that bad?"

"It doesn't feel so. Unless you tell me to go away."

She sat bolt upright, suddenly frightened. "You said you never wanted to claim anyone again. Is that what you've done?"

His expression changed, but he reached up to touch her cheek with a fingertip. "Does that frighten you?"

"Does it frighten me?" Much as she wanted to fall into his arms, she had a bigger concern. She scrambled away from him to the edge of the bed. "It frightened *you.* Why wouldn't it frighten me?"

Now he frowned. "I'm sorry. I have upset you."

"Aren't you upset?"

"Not in the least. Yet."

Oh, this was too much to absorb before she'd even gotten her feet under her. "Did you finish cleaning up the city?"

"We may have another newborn or two to hunt tonight, but as of dawn this morning, no others were left." His frown grew darker. "Dani, what frightens you? That I will follow you everywhere you go? I can swear not to do that."

"So..." She hesitated, confused and very afraid of the answer. "So," she said again, clearing her throat, "you haven't claimed me?"

He sighed. "I think I am messing something up."

"I think I can't think yet. I need coffee. I need to wake up. I'm confused, Luc!"

"The coffee, I can manage. Terri has a passion for it." He slipped from the covers, naked from head to toe, and went to the far corner of the bedroom where a drip coffeemaker stood on a table. "Or maybe I can't manage it. I have never made the stuff."

"Oh, let me." Dani scrambled off the bed and went over. Immediately Luc withdrew, which caused her a sharp pang, but she ignored it while she got the pot going. She rubbed her eyes and turned to find him propped up against pillows in bed, his lower body covered by the comforter.

She stared at him, still trying to comprehend what was going on here. "Did you claim me? Do I have any say?"

"You have every say. Sadly, I am the one who has none. For me it is done."

"Oh." She furrowed her brow, then forced herself to smooth it for fear he might mistake her expression as anger. "How did it happen?"

"It just does. I felt it coming, but I could not walk away."

"Because of the rogues."

"Because of *you.*"

"Oh." Well, that didn't feel so bad, she thought. "Have you eaten? Should I get you a bag?"

A snort that was almost a laugh escaped him. "I am neither sick nor weak. Nor am I injured. What I am is in agony."

Oh, she didn't like the sound of that at all. "Agony? Why?" She stepped toward him, her impulse to help in any way she could. She couldn't stand the thought of him hurting.

"Because I am—how do you say?—on tenterhooks, awaiting your disposal of me."

"Disposal?" She didn't like that word. She drew even closer. Behind her the coffeepot burbled.

"Disposal," he repeated. "I have offered myself. I love you. If you don't want me, you will never see me again."

"What would you do?"

He shrugged.

But she knew. He had told her as much when he had explained claiming. Now that he had claimed her, if she didn't want him, he would…well, she couldn't bear to even think of it.

"You are under no obligation," he said quietly. "I have survived this before."

Barely, she thought, remembering the things he had said. Barely.

"All that matters now," he continued, "is what *you* want, *ma belle.*"

She drew another step closer. Her heart thudded

now, not the rapid patter of fear, but the heavy drumbeat of something very important.

"Are you sure?" she asked. "Really sure? Because, well..." She couldn't say it.

"Because you've been rejected often enough? You don't want to risk it again. Of course I am sure, Dani. I have never been more certain of anything. I only question whether it is good for you and whether you want it. I am, after all, a vampire. You were raised to loathe my kind. Being with me would change your entire life, even if I don't change you. You can never have a child, for one thing."

"Newborns aren't exactly something I want."

He laughed, but it didn't sound quite humorous. "I would be jealous. I would not share you. I would never leave your side except for the briefest of periods. Can you stand that much of me?"

The reality had begun to sink home. Comprehension was arriving. Dani felt herself melt inside and her knees began to turn to rubber.

"Luc..." Then it hit. Fully. A sudden strength filled her limbs and she hurled herself at him. His arms caught her from the air and drew her tight and close.

"Are you sure?" he asked.

"I will be every bit as jealous," she warned him. "I'll want to be with you every minute."

"Ah." His eyes began to lighten to that incredible gold as tension seeped from his body. "So you feel good with me?"

"For the first time in a long time, I feel like I'm home."

His expression lightened with delight. "You cannot know how happy that makes me."

"I love you," she said. "I really, really do."

He cradled her face with one hand. "Be sure. Because if I take this last step, there will be no going back for me. None."

"You're going to change me?"

"No. Not until I am very certain that you are very certain. But I want to make love to you and drink from you at the same time. In that instant, we will truly become one. I will no longer be able to entertain a single thought of life without you."

"I don't want a life without you."

He looked deeply into her eyes. Then, just as she was wondering what he was deciding, he slipped her nightgown over her head and covered her nakedness with his own.

She should have felt shy or nervous, but all she felt was an incredible sense of freedom. She had chosen her path, and it felt so right.

He kissed her deeply, then followed that kiss with more all over her body until she was melted and cried his name. Only then did he slide up over her.

She gasped as he entered her. No one had ever claimed her that way before, and there was a brief searing pain.

"It will pass, *mon amour,* it will pass."

It did as he kissed her again, driving everything

out of her mind but the bliss of being filled by the one she loved.

He moved gently at first, testing, but her body responded as if it had been waiting for this moment to burst free of its bonds. It ignited as if she were gasoline touched by a match. Reaching out, she grabbed his shoulders and arched up against him, demanding more.

His head lowered to her neck. He licked her, coolness against her heated skin. She never felt the prick of his teeth, but she knew the instant it happened.

Suddenly they were one again, hearts beating in unison, pleasure careening through them. She felt his as if it were hers, a rhythm of such intensity and power that she wasn't sure she could bear it.

But she bore it. She held his head close as he drank, felt as if a hot wire of need ran from his mouth to the place where he entered her and moved. She was his and he was hers, and together they climbed to paradise as one.

She had been fully claimed.

* * * * *

PARANORMAL

Dark and sensual paranormal romance stories
that stretch the boundaries of conflict and desire, life and death.

nocturne™

COMING NEXT MONTH
AVAILABLE MARCH 27, 2012

#133 THE WEREWOLF'S WIFE
Michele Hauf

#134 WARRIOR RISING
The Esri
Pamela Palmer

Taft Bowman knew he'd ruined any chance he'd had for happiness with Laura Pendleton when he drove her away years ago...and into the arms of another man, thousands of miles away. Now she was back, a widow with two small children...and despite himself, he was starting to believe in second chances.

Harlequin Special® Edition® presents a new installment in USA TODAY *bestselling author RaeAnne Thayne's miniseries,* THE COWBOYS OF COLD CREEK.

Enjoy a sneak peek of A COLD CREEK REUNION

Available April 2012 from Harlequin® Special Edition®

A younger woman stood there, and from this distance he had only a strange impression, as though she was somehow standing on an island of calm amid the chaos of the scene, the flashing lights of the emergency vehicles, shouts between his crew members, the excited buzz of the crowd.

And then the woman turned and he just about tripped over a snaking fire hose somebody shouldn't have left there.

Laura.

He froze, and for the first time in fifteen years as a firefighter, he forgot about the incident, his mission, just what the hell he was doing here.

Laura.

Ten years. He hadn't seen her in all that time, since the week before their wedding when she had given him back his ring and left town. Not just town. She had left the whole damn country, as if she couldn't run far enough to

HSEEXP0412

get away from him.

Some part of him desperately wanted to think he had made some kind of mistake. It couldn't be her. That was just some other slender woman with a long sweep of honey-blond hair and big, blue, unforgettable eyes. But no. It was definitely Laura. Sweet and lovely.

Not his.

He was going to have to go over there and talk to her. He didn't want to. He wanted to stand there and pretend he hadn't seen her. But he was the fire chief. He couldn't hide out just because he had a painful history with the daughter of the property owner.

Sometimes he hated his job.

Will Taft and Laura be able to make the years recede...or is the gulf between them too broad to ever cross?

Find out in
A COLD CREEK REUNION
Available April 2012 from Harlequin® Special Edition®
wherever books are sold.

Celebrate the 30th anniversary
of Harlequin® Special Edition® with a bonus story
included in each Special Edition® book in April!

Harlequin
Blaze
red-hot reads